William Sharswood

The Betrothed, or, Love in Death

A play in five acts

William Sharswood

The Betrothed, or, Love in Death
A play in five acts

ISBN/EAN: 9783337105488

Printed in Europe, USA, Canada, Australia, Japan

Cover: Foto ©Andreas Hilbeck / pixelio.de

More available books at **www.hansebooks.com**

THE BETROTHED

OR

LOVE IN DEATH

A

PLAY

IN FIVE ACTS

BY

WILLIAM SHARSWOOD A. M. Ph. D. (Jena)

HONORARY MEMBER OF THE GEOLOGICAL SOCIETY OF EDINBURGH NON
RESIDENT MEMBER OF THE SYRO-EGYPTIAN SOCIETY OF LONDON
CORRESPONDENT OF THE IMPERIAL GEOLOGICAL INSTITUTE OF
VIENNA FOREIGN MEMBER OF THE BOTANICAL SOCIETY
OF EDINBURGH AND CORRESPONDING MEMBER OF
THE BOTANICAL SOCIETY OF CANADA OF THE
BOSTON SOCIETY OF NATURAL HISTORY
OF THE ACADEMY OF SCIENCE OF
ST. LOUIS AND MEMBER OF THE
BERWICKSHIRE NATURALISTS'
CLUB

PHILADELPHIA
ASHMEAD & EVANS 724 CHESTNUT STREET
MDCCCLXV

PHILADELPHIA:
PRINTED BY KING & BAIRD, 607 SANSOM STREET.

TO

ALOIS AUER VON WELSBACH

Knight of the Imperial Austrian Orders of the Iron Crown and Francis Joseph
One of his Imperial Apostolic Majesty's Court Counsellors
Director of the Imperial and Royal Court and State Press
Member of the Imperial Academy of Science of Vienna

As a slight but most sincere token of his talents

Profound respect for his character

And as an occasion

For thus publicly acknowledging the obligations under which.

His favoritism has placed the Author

This fruit
Of a desire for contributing to the Legitimate English Drama

IS INSCRIBED

The unworthy performance which is inscribed to you is entitled

THE BETROTHED OR LOVE IN DEATH

PHILADELPHIA, 26 *December*, 1862.

I N publifhing the following Drama, I fhould remark that the plot may be confidered as having no foundation in hiftory, nor as being borrowed from the romance, excepting a *portion* of the *epifode* in the *firft fcene* of the *fourth act*, the incidents of which have been very freely taken from the French of Alphonfe Karr, though the characters have been entirely re-caft.

The author has endeavored in every inftance to approach if not to rigidly preferve the three unities of

action, time, and place, fo far as he thought confiftent
with fcenic reprefentation; conceiving, with the few of
the eligible authors of the more modern fchool, any dif-
tant departure from fuch a courfe to be unadvifable, if at
all admiffible in a drama in any way adapted, or intended
for the ftage.   In this connection it is quite fatiffactory to
know that the unity of time and place, after having been
ftrongly adhered to in the Greek and Roman Theatre,
inculcated by the mediæval fchool, and fubfequently ad-
mitted more or lefs as a matter of tafte, rather than an
opinion of judgment, has been fubfequently infifted on by
certain of the Continental-European critics of Dramatic
propriety as one of the moft effential criterions for the
legitimate Drama.

It is of no ufe to hold out the example of certain un-
approachably fucceffful predeceffors, who wrote without
any definite or regular formation of ftructure, as any
reafon for an utter abandonment of any and all rules.   If
the Drama is an Art, it muft be fubjected to the ufage of
art, and become fubmiffive to rule.   It is quite certain,
however, that even Shakefpeare deviated from an obfervance of the unities through ignorance of their exiftence,
rather than rejected them by defign, if we confider his
leaft methodical performances, however perfect in all
thofe effects derivable from a knowledge of focial nature,
as the productions of his earlier years, when he may
reafonably be fuppofed to have written his leaft method-

ical pieces ; while he may have produced thofe* charac
terized by a nicer obfervance of rule at the period of
his more matured judgment.

The faults of the Play I do not pretend to fet forth,
or defend; trufting, if the performance be worthy of fair
and juft criticifm, they may be found elfewhere.

I am aware that this is a period when the ftage, or
rather the public tafte which rules the ftage, is too fenfa-
tional and melo-dramatic to admit of the expectation of a
fchool, bafed on the nobler paffions alone, becoming popu-
lar in theatrical reprefentation ; a fchool which has for its
higher effects the exhibition of moral beauty and fitnefs,
rather than the reprefentation of the viler paffions, and
the accumulation of everything hideous, revolting, in-

---

* "Of thefe, [The Tempeft, Midfummer Night's Dream, Macbeth and
Hamlet,] The Tempeft, however, it comes to be placed the firft by the pub-
lifhers of his works, can never have been the firft written by him : it feems
to me as perfect in its kind, as almoft anything we have of his.   One may
obferve, that the unities are kept here, with an exactnefs uncommon to the
liberties of his writing; though that was what, I fuppofe, he valued himfelf
leaft upon fince his excellencies were all of another kind."   Some account
of the Life of Mr. William Shakefpeare, written by Mr. [Nicholas] Rowe.

Coleridge formed the fame opinion from different data.   He judged from
the redundancy of double epithets occurring in Love's Labour Loft, Romeo
and Juliet, Venus and Adonis and Lucrece, compared with their difcre-
tionary ufe in Lear, Macbeth, Othello and Hamlet of this dramatift, that
the former were the earlier productions, as he attributes this defect to young
authors.   (Biographia Literaria, Ch. I., *firft foot note.*)   This reafoning
would feem to difcard the claim of The Tempeft to a chronological prece-
dence in the arrangement of his plays, and not only not militate againft
but ftrongly corroborate the ftatement of Rowe.

decent, and confequently reprehenfible to morals, difguft-
ful to tafte, and difgraceful to art, however attractive to
an audience of the prefent day. It is, therefore doubtlefs,
that the prefent attempt may be confidered defective from
the very abfence of the diftinguifhing qualities of the latter
fchool.

I am, moreover, confident that a production like this,
written folely with the view to reprefentation, however ill
adapted it may prove to be, can have but little intereft
for the clofet, and in view of this my feelings may be anti-
cipated by the conviction that the undoubted faults of
the play—at beft a meagre example of the power that the
fyftem is capable of producing in the hands of thofe
who may be immeafurably more fitted for performing the
tafk—fhould be attributed to the failure of the architect
rather than the peculiar fyftem which he has ventured
to illuftrate and defend.

W. S.

PHILADELPHIA, *February*, 1862.*

* I fhould reconcile an apparent difcrepancy between the date of the Preface
(February, 1862), and that attached to the title page (1865), by ftating,
that, after an edition in quarto of the Play, embodying certain philobiblian
taftes, had been carried on through the firft act in 1862, it was fufpended
indefinitely: and the prefent edition of a limited number of copies has been
executed in anticipation of the publication, at a future day, of another
edition, with fuch emendations as the mellowing hand of time may fuggeft.

PHILADELPHIA, *May 1ft*, 1865.

THE BETROTHED

OR

LOVE IN DEATH

TIME DURING WHICH EACH ACT IS SUPPOSED TO TAKE PLACE.

ACT I.—The Night of the firſt day.

ACT II.—The Evening of the ſecond day.

ACT III.—The Noon of the third day.

ACT IV.—The Evening of the fourth day.

ACT V.— $\begin{cases} \text{Sc. 1.—The Evening of the fifth day.} \\ \text{Sc. 2 and 3.—The Night of the fifth day.} \end{cases}$

CORRECTIONS.

ACT II, line 55, *for* throwing pebbles *read* throwing a pebble.

ACT II, line 57, *after* circle, *insert* each.

ACT III, line 140, *for* was as dear *read* am and have been as dear.

ACT IV, line 267, *for* jointed *read* tri-jointed.

ACT V, line 286, *for* giving *read* given.

DRAMATIS PERSONÆ.

MEN.

Count MANDERSTEM, God Father of Levangeline,
Appears ACT i, Sc. 3 : ACT ii, Sc. 4.
FREDERICK Baron DIETRICHSTEIN.
Appears ACT i, Sc. 1, 3 ; ACT ii, Sc. 1, 4; ACT v, Sc. 1, 2.
ALEXANDER Baron WIED.
Appears ACT i, Sc. 1, 3 ; ACT ii, Sc. 1, 2, 4; ACT iii, Sc. 1 ;
ACT v, Sc. 1, 3.
NICHOLAS Count TERTSKY.
Appears ACT ii, Sc. 4 ; ACT iii, Sc. 1 ; ACT iv, Sc. 1.
FRANCIS Count RETSKY.
Appears ACT i, Sc. 3; ACT ii, Sc. 1, 4; ACT iii, Sc. 2 ;
ACT iv, Sc. 2 ; ACT v, Sc. 1, 2.
Friar WILLIAM. *Appears* ACT v, Sc. 2, 3.
MICHAEL valet de Chambre to ALEXANDER.
Appears ACT i, Sc. 1, 2; ACT ii, Sc. 3 ; ACT iv, Sc. 1 ; ACT
v, Sc. 2.
ALFRED valet de Chambre to FREDERICK.
Appears ACT i, Sc. 1, 2 ; ACT ii, Sc. 3 ; ACT v, Sc. 2.
Butler. *Appears* ACT v, Sc. 2.
Five Muſicians. *Appear* ACT ii, Sc. 3.
An attendant on the Muſicians. *Appears* ACT ii, Sc. 3.
Highwayman. *Appears* ACT i, Sc. 2.
Street Watch. *Appears* ACT i, Sc. 2.
Meſſenger. *Appears* ACT iii, Sc. 1.
Two Friars. *Appear* ACT v, Sc. 3.
ARNOLD, ⎫
PHILIP, ⎬ and other Chamois Huntſmen, and Boys.
JOHN, ⎭   *Appear* ACT iv, Sc. 1.
Lords. *Appear* ACT i, Sc. 1.
Friars and Choriſters. *Appear* ACT iv, Sc. 1.
Pages and Servants. *Appear* ACT i, Sc. 3.

WOMEN.

LEVANGELINE Counteſs MANDERSTEM.
Appears ACT i, Sc. 3 ; ACT ii, Sc. 2, 4 ; ACT iii, Sc. 1 ; ACT
iv, Sc. 2 ; ACT v, Sc. 1, 3.
JOSEPHINE, friend of Levangeline. *Appears* ACT i, Sc. 3.
EULALIE. *Appears* ACT i, Sc. 3.
CLARA. *Appears* ACT i, Sc. 3.
IDA, attendant on Levangeline. *Appears* ACT i, Sc. 3 ; ACT iii,
Sc. 1 ; ACT iv, Sc. 1 ; ACT v, Sc. 1.
Ladies. *Appear* ACT i, Sc. 3.
Hunters' Wives. *Appear* ACT iv, Sc. 1.

SCENE.—Auſtria on the borders of the Styrian Alps.

COSTUMES.

COUNT MANDERSTEM.—*Firſt dreſs:* Purple or lilac colored velvet dreſs, richly trimmed with gold embroidery. *Second dreſs:* Looſe fitting ſuit.

ALEXANDER BARON WIED.—*Firſt dreſs:* Full court dreſs, chapeau and ſword. *Second dreſs:* According to taſte of actor.

FREDERICK BARON DIETRICHSTEIN.—*First dreſs:* Full evening dreſs, with decoration, chapeau and ſword. *Second dreſs:* According to taſte of actor.

NICHOLAS COUNT TERTSKY.—After the ſtyle of Alexander's firſt dreſs.

FRANCIS COUNT RETSKY.—Looſe frock coat, black cloth cap and oſtrich plumes, ſilk ſaſh decoration and ſword.

Friar WILLIAM.—Grey gown, girdle and ſandals.

MICHAEL.—Blue livery, with metal buttons; red waiſtcoat; knee breeches of ſame; white party-colored ſtockings; ſmall top boots; French cap, with leather front.

ALFRED.—Drab colored doublet and pantaloons, ruſſet boots and round cap.

Street Watch.—Grey frock, numbered on the left breaſt; long leather apron; black gaiters, and large tin hat, turned up in front, à l'Eſpagnol, marked by letters and characters; with a leather baſket thrown over the ſhoulders, ſuſpended to a belt, à la militaire; long pole or ſtaff tipped with iron.

Butler.—Brown coat, ſcarlet veſtcoat, black breeches, ſtriped ſtockings, ſhoes, buckles.

Chamois Huntſmen.—Dark jackets; pantlets of ſame color, ſupported by leather belts; worſted ſtockings; ſhoes, buckles and felt hat; long climbing ſtaffs finiſhed with an iron point at one end, and with a hook at the other end.

LEVANGELINE COUNTESS MANDERSTEM.—*Firſt dreſs:* White ſatin dreſs with ſtraw-colored ſilk bodice and train, richly embroidered with gold and ſilver. *Second dreſs:* Plain white muſlin. *Third dreſs:* Blue ſilk. *Fourth dreſs:* According to taſte of actreſs. *Fifth dreſs:* Plain white muslin wrapper. *Sixth dreſs:* Rich white ſatin dreſs with a purple or lilac robe embroidered with gold.

IDA.—Slate colored robe trimmed with black velvet.

JOSEPHINE.—*Firſt dreſs:* White ſilk, trimmed with amber or ſtraw-colored ſilk. *Second dreſs:* According to the taſte of actreſs.

EULALIE.—⎫
CLARA.—⎬ Similar to Joſephine's firſt dreſs.

THE BETROTHED;

OR,

LOVE IN DEATH.

ACT I.

Scene 1.—*An apartment in the house of Frederick the Baron von Dietrichstein. Time Night, Frederick seated, (R. C.) musing over a letter and medallion. He paces the stage a few times and pauses (R. C.) as in a reverie.*

FREDERICK.

AS it even so, then, Cleomira?
  Thou didst love me!—and I too secretly
  Worshipped thee! Thou didst love me
      to suffering!—
And still with a passion unknown to me!—   5
Thou, whose love might call into life
The very images thou look'st upon
Within yon dim cloister'd cell ; and cause their
Sculptured veins to beat with animation !
All's now vain joy and thirst insatiable,   10
As is the glist'ning lizard's form, basking
In sunshine, to the bruised serpent's eye,

Powerless from its impotence of power!— *[Crossing* L.
But must I be blamed for the tenderness
Which took possession of her lab'ring heart,
15 And caused her to put on rigid convent vows
Not to bleach anew her sordid breast, for
It ever was immaculate?—Rather
Say innocent—yet not entirely so.

Enter ALFRED, L.

Alf (L. c.) The Baron von Wied presents his duty
20 To your lordship, and waits without.
　　Fred. (*Taken by surprise.*)　　　　Have you
Correctly carried the title?
　　Alf.　　　　　　　　'Twas thus,
Your lordship, I read the card.
25　　*Fred.*　　　　　　　　I'm at home,
To his lordship.　　　　　　　　*[Exit* ALFRED.
　　Fred.　　　But two days at most elapsed
Since I had his accustomed fortnight's letter
Of such contents as leads me to suspect
30 He'd not thought of this unlooked for visit.

Enter ALEXANDER, C. *from* L.

Alexander, is it you, my dear friend?　　*[They embrace.*
　　Alex. Frederick, it is!—It is the same that
Three years ago and more, went forth endowed
By our native Austria's peerless realm,
35 With an official charge to a distant court,—
The same that bade farewell, within these halls,
To friendship, born and nurtured in childhood's
Early acquaintance.
　　Fred.　　　　'Tis true. A friendship
40 Not revived, since it has ne'er been broken,
Is worth the cherishing.
　　Alex.　　　　'Tis like the proved blade
Which breaks ere it yields to a second power.
　　Fred. I'm glad to find you so content with that
45 In youth and childhood hath been our home.

Alex. I am so, Frederick; the memories of
The days long since gone by, crowd on my mind,
When I could think so fondly on trivial things,
As to imagine a heaven of happiness
From free indulgence of those appetites   50
That have now cloyed with satiety;
When the sun scarce left the noontide's angle,
Than graver duties gave way to mirthful sports—
The hazy lake, where it hath been our pleasure
To drift along as lightly as a leaf,   55
Dropping here and there our breeze-swollen lines,
With the varying fortune of the sport—
Those dear old trees and circumambient walks,
Where we've emulated each the other
In the courser's speed—and other pastimes   60
That summed up the wealth of youthful pleasure.
    Fred. There's nothing in what the world calls pleasure
But is common to the attributes of
Knowledge, power, and love. What can be reckoned
Pleasure after love? As the sleek hound which   65
Hath once tasted blood, the heart can ne'er be
Sated with aught else.
I wish at times this world or life was over:
Nought happens when we come of reason's age,
But is a reproduction of the ceaseless,   70
Changeless, hopeless round through which we have passed
In childhood's days.
And most we wish ne'er happens, but much more
Of trial and disaster than we counted on,
Displaces pleasure with a sad relief.   75
    Alex. Frederick! There's something altered in that
       face ;—
'Tis not the same I left three years ago.
    Fred. All things show unto me their darkest sides,
And nought enchains me longer to the earth.
    Alex. I see confession in thy countenance.   80
                                  [*Crosses,* R.
Forget the scenes around you. Meantime,
My friendship shall prove more than wordy vaunting;
And believe you, hope will yet plan anew
The road to full accomplishment.

85   *Fred.*   Dost thou remember,
The legend of Italy's laureled bard,
Spoken by the eternal doomed souls in hell,
"Only so far afflicted, that we live
Desiring without hope?"*   Where hope comes not,
90   Is death; and what have I to longer hope.

                                    [*Crosses,* L.
Press me no further.   What brings you hither?
If 'tis a cause no excess of modesty
Forbids thee to divulge, unbosom thee,
And prove thy confidence above wordy vaunting.
95   My friendship would scarce be worth the keeping,
Should I appear incurious of your
Inmost secrets.
        Alex.   Thou mightst have judged, by
The accustomed quickness of thy apprehension,
100   That the cause might be——
            Fred.   A lady?
            Alex.   You smile.
        Fred. Dost thou recall the tale thou oft hast told—
Nought but ambition's course you'd e'er pursue;
105   But time, the unerring interpreter
Of man's acts, as actions are of his thoughts,
Has thus disproved thy claim to rightful judgment.
        Alex. 'Tis not by heav'n granted, that our lives should
Always be directed by our wishes.
        Fred. I would not have thee turn tell-tale of thy
110   heart,
And vows of her that may be doubly sacred;
But so much of the lady's quality,
And of the occurrence of thy meeting,
As befits thy willingness to unfold,
115   I would gladly learn.
        Alex.   Her name and station—
'Twere best to say I can't divulge at present.
        Fred. Quite explicit so far—pray you proceed—
How long since you first declared your passion?
120   *Alex.* The night of the day on which we first met.

---

* Che senza speme vivemo in dis'o.—
            DANTE, *L'Inferno*, Canto IV.

Fred. The night of the day on which you first met ?—
But the occasion——
    Alex.   Hear, then, I'll tell thee :
'Twas at a Parisian banquet, to which
The lady, from this distance had been asked.—   125
In a balcony we were standing mute,
Except in aspects that speak more than words,
And looking out upon the star-pearled heav'n,
As if to take a breath of fresh'ning air ;
I longed that we might have a little star,   130
Where we might dwell unknown but to ourselves ;
Where unknown bliss should nestle round our hearts,
And all creation seem happy for our sakes.
She faltered : the silver hue of night was hid,
But soon breaking through a fleecy cloudlet,   135
Relieved the glowing blushes on her cheeks ;
I took her hand in mine, my lips touched hers ;
The magic touch cemented both our hearts together ;
We heard a rustling in the room close by,
Which parted us.   140
    Fred.   You saw her soon again ?
    Alex. What since has crossed her thoughts I'm
               stranger to,
Content to know her beaming eyes bespoke
The meaning of her soul. Dost know our friend
Count Manderstem gives a banquet to-night ?   145
    Fred. Yes ; and all that are known to him as friends
Have been invited.
    Alex.   A thought has struck me ;
Would'st have with me to your uncle's mansion ?
More than thou thinkst of may there be witnessed   150
Of that which besteads me to keep secret.
Wilt join me then ?
    Fred.   I will !
    Alex.   Have thither now !
               [*Exeunt,* c. D.
Alf. (*Without,* L.) Hurry on, boys, hurry on.   155

Enter ALFRED, L.

Alf. (L.) For these three months master hasn't gone

into company, and scarcely has a smile wrinkled his
face—when of a sudden, he gives me orders to follow his
steps with agility. Now I don't like doing things with
160 agility, for when one tries to do things better or quicker
than he can, he always does them the worse.

Enter MICHAEL, c. *from* L,

Who is there ?
   Mich. It's only myself. I have the honor to introduce
myself the valet to his lordship the Baron Alexander
165 Wied, secretary to his most faithful Majesty's Envoy-
Extraordinary and Minister Plenipotentiary to the Court
of Paris. My master told me that your master had
asked him to tell me to tell you, that I should have myself
in readiness to join you.
170   *Alf.* (*Observing a rent in* MICHAEL'S *stocking.*) What's
this ?
   Mich. I pray your pardon, the cause is this—as I was
leaving the lodge, the usher bade me beware of the quadruped within the walls, as he had a taste for muscle,
175 and as I thought myself to be nigh the doors, I mistook
my path and came on the meat house, when the animal
taking me for some straggler seized me by my ankle, and
destroyed this stocking.
   Alf. What is that ?
180   *Mich.* What is that !—These stockings were left to
my father by his father, when he fled from France to
Spitalsfields on the revocation of the Edict of Nantes,
for no better generosity that he couldn't take them with
him.
185   *Alf.* Mercy on us—mercy on us—I most forgot what
I have to do.   [*Exit* ALFRED, L.
   Mich. Now I must be preparing to wait on my master,
but first of all I'll take a look to see how the streets run
in these quarters. (*Goes up to window* L., *and opens it ;*
190 *dog heard without.*) Oh ! (*Clasping his ears, and closing
the window. Approaches the window,* R., *and opens it :
dog heard.*) This must be the triple-headed dog of
Hades. It's very hard to lose a nether stock (*looking at
his foot,*) of such as were left to my grandsire, by one

that fled his home on the revocation of the Edict of
Nantes, for no better generosity than he couldn't take   195
them with him.

Re-enter ALFRED, C. D.

Alf. What would you?
Mich. Now for the outfits of my master.
                                  [*Exit* ALFRED, C. D.
I'm not right yet.   [*Ringing the bell.*

Re-enter ALFRED, L.

First of all, for fear you should fall, let me have the cha-   200
peau ; and next in order let me have the sword ; however,
to save your steps, just call in your badgers.
Alf. Here Peter, George, John.

Enter SERVANT *with a chapeau, C. D., and one attendant,
with a sword, L., and another with a box, R.*

Alf. I must tell you as a stranger in these parts, that
it's very needful for you to be at least guarded by a   205
pistol, if you wish to take the shortest road round to the
count's.
Mich. I never yet received from mortal man an injury,
but I paid back with threefold interest before demand.
Alf. Where's your means?   210
Mich. I'm a peace commissioner,—yet I always carry
my pistol in my pocket. (*Taking out a flask:*) And
now you are to see me safe through these grounds : you
taking the lead,—and you the aft,—and you to the side
nearing the quadruped. Well now, each keep his proper   215
distance.   [*Exeunt.— The dog heard without.*

SCENE II.—*A Street in a dilapidated part of the Town.*

Enter MICHAEL, L., *covered with a cloak, carrying a chapeau box, and sword ; who is met by a Highwayman,
with a dark lantern, that has entered from a house,* L. C

Highw. (*Accosting.*) Ho, there, neighbour ! you'll not
mistrust my penury when I demand five florins.

Mich. What's that to me?

Highw. (*Unperceived seizes* MICHAEL *by the coat collar with one hand, and brandishes a knife before him with the*
220 *other hand.*) My demand, or your life on it.

Mich. Hold, hold, let's reason! (*Aside.*) I must dissemble to my best. (*Aloud.*) You're not going to deny my claim to a partnership in your art—don't you perceive in me one of your company—what luck has been to you
225 to-day?

Highw. Why none at all—and just as I thought to have my game in you——

Mich. You found us both bait together.

Highw. Yes, my good fellow. Come in and have
230 a look over my last haul.

Mich. The next time that I am passing—the next time——

Highw. But I never plant my stakes twice in the same place. I always remove before any danger is at hand ;—
235 when the authorities are ready to search one house, I shift my quarters to the nearest at hand, and thus keep just near enough to my enemies to know my danger. Come in, come in.

Mich. The next time. (*Aside.*) If he should trap me in
240 the end, I'm lost.

Highw. But you'll not think me generous till I empty a bottle between us at my own expense.

Mich. No, thank you,—thank you. I have too much consideration for your art, to indulge in such an extrava-
245 gance at your cost ;—but instead of it, you can do me a favor in another way.

Highw. What is it?

Mich. You'll not mistake me the next time we meet?

Highw. Oh, no—we're in bonded brotherhood hereafter.
                [*Going towards the door.*
250   *Mich.* Yes, remember, in bonded brotherhood.
                [*Exit Highwayman by the door,* L. C.
Voices, (*within.*) Halves, halves!

Mich. An adventure well played out—boarded and brought to within a hand's grasp,—the third mishap this night: if this be the aspect of my lordship's town,
255 it was never made for peace commissioners. How-

ever, I'll make profit of this occasion to publish my
card in the " Staats Zeitung," as Michael Cabalé, valet de
chambre to his lordship, Alexander the Baron von Wied,
one of the secretaries of his Majesty's Minister Plenipotentiary and Envoy Extraordinary at the Court of Paris.   260
I'll note the house, and have the notice headed, " Wanton
Act of Violence on strangers, and outrage on peace commissioners ! Robbery on the highways by moonlight !"
I'll have it ushered in by a profusion of marks of ex-
clamation fore and aft, and with an illustration taken by   265
their eye witness artist.   It's lucky he did not ask, nay
more, demand a sight of my supposed, but his mistaken,
spoils.   However, I'll be going,—my nerves begin to
shake, my limbs to quake, anon my very bones to crack ;
it must be a low-land part of the town ; I use to be a fit   270
subject for the ague.   (*Taking a drink from his flask.*)
I'm a peace commissioner.   Peace be to my followers.
                                                    [*Exit,* L.

Enter WATCHMAN, L., *running in search of the Highwayman and meeting* ALFRED *takes him for the man.*

Watchm. I'll take my stand for you.

                    Enter ALFRED, R.

Watchm. What calls you hither ?
Alf. I'm the attendant of my good and noble master,   276
von Dietrichstein.
Watchm. Then show me your mark, if you serve his
lordship, before I give the pass.
Alf. Here it be.   [*Showing the name-plate on the sword.*
Watch. Pass on,—you are not my man.   280
                    [*Exit,* R., *rapping thrice with his staff.*
Alf. He's taken me so aback, I've most forgotten to
note the spot of this my first adventure. (*Looking about.*)
Oh, yes, it's opposite Nick Bogg's home for stragglers.
If Michael be safe through, it proves the force of diplo-
macy against arms, ammunition, and belligerent sway.   285
                                                    [*Exit,* L.

Scene III.—*A magnificent apartment, lighted up with festal splendor, in the mansion of the Count Manderstem; in the rear, two folding doors opening into another saloon, with a table elegantly supplied with viands, c., and servants in waiting; the centre doors of the second saloon, which are standing open, gives to the prospect a view of the hall containing statuary and other works of art. The whole having the appearance of a banquet advanced close on to the dawn of day.*

Alexander *and* Levangeline *discovered on a couch,* R., *engaged in conversation. On the side directly opposite,* Frederick, *by himself, apparently lost in thought, and taking no part in any thing that is going on. The middle space between the Proscenium, at some distance from the edge of the stage, is filled up by the* Count, Francis, Josephine, Eulalie, *and* Clara. *A portion of the company are promenading, some are examining the works of art, and others seated throughout the apartments.*

Count. (c.) 'Tis late, 'tis late; the golden hue of dawn
Streaks through the lattice upon our moping lights.
It is a lovely scene; but good, my friends,
The sun reproves us for our lengthened merriment,
290   And, jealous of his matchless state, will teach
That pleasure waxes heavy towards the morn; [*Crosses,* L.
Then let what remains, of this full late hour,
Be eked out in pleasures, as brilliant as
This morn's onsetting dawn can happy greet.
295   We'll think no more there's aught of earthly ills,
Where power, beauty, love, wit, wealth, and wine
Earth's chiefest pleasures, supremely reign.
The sprightly bowl once more shall be refilled,
And as we pass it gaily round—drink deep—
300   Filling again and emptying the same
At each toast, as it goes merrily round.   [*Crosses,* R.
I'll first command, that each may do the most
What most each likes, which each that thinks ay
        with me,
Will signify by emptying his glass.—

Resume the dance, your instruments advance,   305
　　　　　　　　　　[*Crosses*, c.
Sound the trumpet, inspire the octave flute,
And let the cords to their own measures bend :—
Bid ev'ry note of harmony awake,
To beat down sorrow, and assuage trial.

[*A portion of the company arrange themselves in the attitude
of the Minuet; the Orchestra plays the music of the
Minuet; in the course of which flashes of lightning are
seen, and peals of thunder heard.* EULALIE *falters,
pauses, and faints in* FRANCIS' *arms; the Minuet is
broken up in the utmost confusion. All exeunt,* c., *except* ALEXANDER *and* LEVANGELINE.

　Lev. (*To* ALEXANDER.) Nay, do not go, but linger yet
　　awhile,   310
We'll not be missed among the gay throng.
　Alex. I'll nor go, nor stay, except thou will'st it so.
　Lev. Then sit, and I will teach myself to thee.
Last night I dreamt that thou had'st loved me,—
And, then, alas ! that thou had'st something proved——   315
　Alex. Love's oft end, falsehood more or less, I judge.
　Lev. Though it pains me much, I can't dissuade the
　　truth,
That methought I was not thy only love,
But still resolved to love thee, till this heart
As flesh in dust lies adamantine cold.   320
　Alex. Nay, I love thee, and will never leave thee,
Till death's dark veil shall hide me from thy face,
And then methinks, my soul would stay with thee !
　Lev. Wilt swear to that ?
　Alex.　　　　　　Ay, by any oath you'll frame.   325
If earth can from its circled orb be turned,
And leave the Sun, and he in turn the zones,
If yon clustered stars, that mark the North,
Can leave their rightly appointed places,
Dark'ning the very spots they once illumined,   330
Bright beguilers to the watchful pilot,
If creation's rule can leave the world,
That it by will ordained hath justly fashioned,

Soul, Sun, Earth, Stars, Creation's rule may part,
335 I shall never from *thee*, Levangeline !
My thoughts, and actions are alone of thee.
  Lev. Most amply, be thy pardon, then ;—
  Alex.   In proof
Whereof our lips to lips thus purge all doubt. [*Kissing.*
340 *Lev.* It is fabled of certain fruits, though touched
By Autumn's searching frosts—when all nature
Seems blossoming with hues of red and gold—
Lose nothing of the tempting color of their rinds,
That are all dust and lothed decay within.
345 Such had I feared to be thy love for me ;—
And when we parted, as e'er since, I felt
A certain aching here, for whose relief
       [*Pointing to her heart.*
Flavia* has long since prescribed despair ;
And to my father's tormenting queries,
350 " What ails thee, child ? look'st never so before"—
I answered that which cast his mind in greater doubt ;
Lest by revealing my true feeling sense,
I should have thine own disclosed.
Now methinks I should have been less open,
355 And feigned to be less captious.
But where on this earth should'st thou look for truth,
If on my tongue thou should'st fail to find it.
  Alex. The thought I ne'er should meet thee more, as
    then
Thou wert, a countess of eighteen summers,
360 And three from out a far distant convent,—
And thy parting glance had such an aspect
Of that, to which your actions testified,
And lacked but confirmation from thy tongue,
Conspired to make me e'er since to languish
365 Till this propitious night.
  Lev.   My own true sense !

   Re-enter FRANCIS *and* CLARA, C. D. *from* L.

Let us retire awhile till these pass on.
   [*Exeunt* ALEXANDER *and* LEVANGELINE, R. S. E.

---

 * On whose gardens George Granville, Lord Lansdown, Baron
Bideford wrote some verses.

Fran. How fortunate am I, who after having visited
so many courts while on my travels, where I have seen
ladies that justly may be called beautiful, but since my.   370
return have met with no one that could bring herself into
comparison with their faces, till I met with one that not
only sums up all the qualities of loveliness in others, but
has that which can only be described as a treasure peculiar to herself.   375

Clar. .These encomiums from such a source, my lord,
have quite overpowered my senses ;—but if, there was a
probability of my being ignorant of my own defects,
so good natured a compliment might of itself give me
graces which I was not possessed of before.   380

Fran. Nay, further—some may be empowered to move
the heart by slow degrees, and others with some one
charm may take the senses captive, but you, my lady,
have that combination of graces which attack and as soon
subdue each faculty at sight.   385

Clar. How unfortunate that I should have studied the
lesson *self* so well, that all the advantage I can gain from
your report, is the honor I have in being in the company of one whose wit can find something to praise in
those so little praiseworthy.   390

Fran. Did I not hear thee address thyself to the look-
ing-glass an hour ago—that it was no wonder that so
many loved thee for thou wert so beautiful.

Clar It was very wrong to overhear me.

Fran. It is worse for thee not to believe it from others.   395

Clar. My lord, I have a trifling favor to gain from
thee.

Fran. (*Kneels.*) Whatever thou wilt.

Clar. Promise me that thou wilt excite extreme jealousy
amongst my rivals, Josephine and Eulalie.   400

Fran. I'll do my best to serve thee in such an inglorious service.

Clar. Inglorious !

Fran. Pardon me, for disloyalty to your royalty, as
thou art my queen to-night.   405

Clar. I have my ideas schooled into a plan. So if it
please thee, come.   [*Exeunt* FRANCIS *and* CLARA, L. S. E.

Re-enter FRANCIS *and* EULALIE, C. *from* R.

Eul. (C.) From whom took'st thou that rose ?
Fran. (C.)　　　　　　　　　　From thee, dearest.
410　'Twas surely wrong to harm the harmless rose,
For to harm it is to harm the one, that
Takes from it so much to make her lovely.
　　Eul. I dread to think how deep thou canst dissemble,
And that too when thou look'st so much devout.
415　*Fran.* For many days I've been striving to learn
The course that should be run by one, that longs
To gain a name amongst the nations ; and
Return to bask in earth's every pleasure,
And fly all but love and thee.
420　*Eul.*　　　　　　　　　　Count Francis,
Thou art far more gallant than faithful.　'Twas
But a moment since I saw thee kneeling
To another, breathing the like false vows.
　　Fran. Why was I formed so passing beautiful,
425　Or women turned such fools, that all must love me,
Else should I not play truant to so many hearts.

[JOSEPHINE *and* CLARA, *who have been occasionally crossing
the stage, in the middle apartment, observing* FRANCIS, *and*
EULALIE, L., *enter in the back ground, and stand* C. JO-
SEPHINE *expresses in her countenance visible signs of
surprise and emotion.*

Jos. (*To* CLARA.) Had I not seen it, I would not have
　　believed it.
Fran. Wilt walk without, dearest ?
Eul.　　　　　　　　　　But the damp air——
430　*Fran.* Will only prove how pleasure may outweigh pain.

[*As he leads her off,* L., JOSEPHINE *comes forward and
accosts him.* EULALIE *exits,* L. S. E., *and* CLARA *withdraws.*

Jos. (L.) Hear ! I came to tell thee something, Francis,
'Tis but to say we part—for ever part.

Fran. Not so, my lady, 'twould be more than death.
Jos. With thee, love is to sue, to gain, deceive ;
And next to tire of, to neglect, and leave. 435
Fran. Cease, fair lady, cease those ill-timed wails ;
And shake those aching sighs from off thine eye-lids ;
Nor let a thought of discord trouble thee :
But may new vows restore the heart once mine.

CLARA *re-enters* C. *from* L., *and* EULALIE, L.

Jos. Thou art ever free to wander here and there, 440
And swear thy love to others as thou hast to me.
Eul. And to me before——
Clar. And again to me.
[CLARA *immediately exits* C. *to* L., *and* EULALIE, L. JOSEPH-
INE *hurries off,* R., *followed by* FRANCIS.

Re-enter ALEXANDER *and* LEVANGELINE, C. *from* L.

Lev. Good night, good night ! sweet repose come o'er thee,
Not as slumber to my languishing eyes, 445
Which thought of thee long has to them denied.
Alex. As the rose is not all flower, but hath much,
If bound into a garland, 'twould tear our brows,
So hope rewards not without some sorrow. [*Going.*
Lev. Pray linger yet a moment. 450
[*Retires to the couch on which she has been seated during
the evening, and returns with a bouquet.*
Alex. (*Aside.*) Would I were
A mote of dust, to float along the air,
As the thin bright gossamer line, which yields
Its flitting movements to the summer's air,
Perchance to light upon that unsunned breast. 455
Lev. To assure thee of my first and only choice
Take this.
Alex. I thank thee truly. (*Cuts a slit in the left breast of
his coat, and inserts the bouquet therein.*) If aught
Has made me blest since first we met, it is 460
In what thou say'st in giving me these flowers ;
For they will teach me how to think of bliss.

As a memento of my faith's vow, take this ;
'Tis of jewels formed that I received
465 From one, who took them from an Ethiop's ear.
[*Takes a ring from off his finger and offers it to* LEVAN-
        GELINE.
A ring fashioned as a serpent coiléd,
Most ancient emblem of eternity.*
The diamond, say a token of our true
Loves' eternal purity.   Take it then.
470 There are no nobler heav'n-born ornaments,
Than the ideas of beauty it calls up,
And just qualities of love it emblems.
        Lev. Why how beautiful !   How cam'st thou by it ?
Some teach that diamonds are of all things purest,
475 Their strength exceeds all others save their own,
But their embodied light by fire consuming,
Renders to earth nought but an empty vapor ;
Such may never be our loves' purity.
        Alex. Jewels are not of all things in my sight,
480 As to the world's enslaved, most precious.

* The form of the serpent coiled into a circle with its tail in its
mouth is one of the most ancient and most significant symbols
devised by the intelligence of man ; even vying with the cross in
antiquity.   Nor was its use confined to any one people, but it
has been employed by nations, as well as painters, sculptors, and
poets.   In Skandinavian Mythology we are told that Loki's
offspring by Angurbodi, a giantess of Jotunheim, were called the
Wolf Fenrir, the Midgard Serpent, and Hela, or Death.   When
the offspring of Loki were born, Odin sent for them, and after
having put the Wolf Fenrir in fetters, threw the Midgard Serpent
into the ocean that encompassed the earth,—here the monster
grew to such an enormity that he encircled the entire earth, with
his tail in his mouth.
    The Egyptians used it as an emblem of the heavens, and its
scales and variegated spots denoted the stars, and was sometimes
used by them as a hieroglyphic of the universe itself.   The tail in
the mouth was expressive of the fact that Time destroys his own
productions, and from this arose its association with the Scythe
in the representations of Saturn, for a symbol of Time and the
revolutions of the year.   It was also used to denote the continuity
or perpetuity of the heavenly motions, and through all time, and
in all places in the Eastern Countries, it was and still remains the
emblem of Eternity.

'Tis in the ends to which they may be turned'
Their value lies, as is ambition's strife
To good ends turned.   Once more adieu !   [*Going.*
    Lev.   Adieu !
Remember what you said about the flowers.   485
    [*Exeunt* ALEXANDER, C. *to* L., *and* LEVANGELINE, C. *to* R.

END OF ACT I.

ACT II.

Scene I.—*A Drawing Room in the House of the* Baron
Dietrichstein, *as before.* Frederick *discovered
seated,* R. C.

Enter Alfred, C. D. *from* R.

Alfred, R. C.

NE waits below, that says your lordship is expecting, but refused me his
name as though I could not bear it
in my memory this distance.

5   *Fred.* Describe his persòn.

    Alf. By his appearance I'd judge
him to be a candidate for philosophy's doctorship.

    Fred. It's none other than Nicholas the Count Roussac,
lately returned from his studies at Jena, the pride of the
10 scholastics, and the victor of more fair hearts in this
last week, than his years amount to. Admit him,—and
further if the Baron Wied should call, have him shown
here.   [*Exit* Alfred, C. D. *off* L.

Enter Francis, C. D. *from* R.

How late you are—I had provided supper at the hour of
15 our engagement the last night.

    Fran. I returned too late from the play, where I had
been induced to go by meeting a friend who was hither
bound, and would have me join him to converse before
the piece commenced.

20   *Fred.* Pray who was there?

    Fran. Opposite me were seated the Baron Wied and
Countess Manderstem.

    Fred. Ah me! there's truly love where I had wished
to find but friendship.

25   *Fran.* Why it would be easier to weigh the earth by

a new invented formula, than to determine the line
'twixt friendship and love between man and woman.

Fred. Which of thy dark lettered tomes has taught thee
this ?

Fran. My midnight reveries, based on my own ex- 30
perience.

Fred. It is quite the hour he should be here.

Fran. I'll be glad to meet him once again, before I
must be back to Jena, to await promotion-day.

Fred. I think I heard his voice without this moment. 35

Enter ALEXANDER, C. D.

How do you ?

Alex. Quite well.

Fran. One's self must least be acquainted, then, with
his own condition.

Alex. How so ? 40

Fran. Well, allow me to prescribe for you.

Alex. First assure me that you know my case.

Fran. I'll take you there,—your heart is the cause
of your distemper ;—I'm glad to be leaving the town so
soon, for it's not yet proved if love be not contagious. 45

Alex. Well, since you have so well merited a hearing
in my case, let us have it.

Fran. Love is but another name for the queen of
charming cares, and while the cherished draught is
in your breast, believe it will ferment, then madden, 50
and after strengthen,—diseased with jealousy, harassed
by absence, distrust, and ever-anxious joys, life's powers
are softened, and you lay dissolved in languor. Get you
to bed this night, and dream of a child upon a gravelly
bank, throwing pebbles into the stream, which first forms 55
a little indentation of its own size, and then circle after
circle, yielding to another larger in turn, until growing
wider and wider, at last is lost in distant view, while the
power and instrument that formed it remain unseen. This
is the dream of fame. 60

Fred. (*To* ALEXANDER.) Does this case apply to you ?

Alex. Too well so, and too far afflicted to prove the
antidote. Let us change the subject. There is news

65 afloat; you told me of the unexpected return of the Count
Tertsky from the embassy at Constantinople, and that he
comes, too, by the mandate of the Count Manderstem.
(*To* FRANCIS.) Have you heard of it?

Fran. I have heard,—(FREDERICK *motions to* FRANCIS *in*
70 *dumb show to keep silence*,) some vague idea of his return
at a distant day.

Alex. What can be the nature of his negotiation with
the Count Manderstem?

Fred. (*As if endeavoring to change his thoughts.*) Ex-
75 cuse my interruption,—but the day has hung very heavy
with me, and I propose that we have some thing to try
our throats.

Fran. I concede to that.

[*Exeunt* ALEXANDER, FREDERICK, *and* FRANCIS.

SCENE II.—*The balcony of* COUNT MANDERSTEM'S *Mansion, with a view of the garden. Time—sunset, with the
Moon in the heavens.*

ALEXANDER *and* LEVANGELINE *enter from the house,* L.

Lev. (*Entering.*) What have you been doing since noon?
80 *Alex.* I've been engaged in busy idleness,—in thinking
of you, and how I could have spent three weeks out of
your sight.

Lev. But you have learned, no doubt, ere this, that
absence strengthens love.
85 *Alex.* It would ne'er strengthen mine. I see you and
leave you each time we meet, as a play-worn child, which
longs for its night of rest, only to languish for its next
day's play in turn. Dost thou still love me, Levangeline?

Lev. Do I still love you!
90 *Alex.* It is surely wrong to question thee thus, Levangeline. But I fear lest thy love may prove flickering or
transient as the bow in the cloud, which while we admire
is lost in vanishment.

Lev. It is unjust to question me in this wise. The
95 only wise thing I ever did was to love thee, nor would I
have another as wise.

Alex. (*After a pause.*) I must be gone, Levangeline.

Lev. That is not just, nor kind. Thou should'st be with none other but me. It was but yesterday, thou said'st thou would'st be with none but me.   100

Alex. Was I not with thee all this morn?

Lev. Thou truly wert: but then——

Alex. But what?

Lev. Often and often, when I looked on thee, thou wast not thinking of me.   .   105

Alex. (*Looking fondly on her.*) Levangeline!

Lev. I know that thou lovest me; and for that reason alone, I cannot bear to think, speak, or look on any one but thee.

Alex I was thinking of a dream.   110

Lev. Pray, what was the subject?

Alex. Love, to be sure.

Lev. Then tell me of it; for if it be something about love, it can't be wrong.

Alex. The details, I have quite forgot.   115

Lev. Reflect a moment!

Alex. I *can't* recall it.

Lev. I don't like this; Thou art not in earnest.

Alex. Well, then, the story is quickly told. There once existed two lovers.   120

Lev. Once! indeed, how strange!—Pray, proceed.

Alex. Their name and place, it is best for the present purpose, to say—that, I forget.

Lev. Say, then, it was *ourselves.*

Alex. That's so personal.   125

Lev. Grant it.

Alex. The lady was, as you would surely grant, most beautiful, and he the same. They used to meet, speak, write, sing, walk, sail upon the waters, care for and look on nothing on earth besides themselves.   130

Lev. Just as all the like would do. Quite natural—so far—pray go on.

Alex. I dare not love.

Lev. Well, then, I will not tire you longer with entreaty.
                    [*Walks aside.*

Alex. Come hither, Levangeline, the evening air is sweet.   135

Lev. Yes, how conducive is this time for love. The

sun falls golden on the dark moor hill, and the moon, now rising slow, beams on the pebble-margined lake, each seeming envious of its proffered light. When all things

140 seem so bright and lovely for our sakes, is it not wrong for *us* not to be happy !

Alex. Would it were ever so !

Lev. What do you mean ?

Alex. I cannot tell.

145 *Lev.* I have no secrets from thee.

Alex. I would the reason was unknown to me.

Lev. Why is every thing you say, this evening, so buried in mystery ?

Alex. To be then as candid, as I have been seemingly

150 dark, Levangeline ! the day may be close at hand, when you shall find a rightful lover, in one whom you have spoken of as a friend. In that is summed the dream, Levangeline.

Lev. Again, you throw these barriers between me and

155 your love.

Alex. It was but a moment since you would know all.

Lev. Well, so I did, for nothing comes to us too soon but ill news,—and I was not thinking of that. The evening breeze chills me.

160 *Alex.* Will you have a mantle ?   [*Going off*, R.

Lev. Yes—oh, no, I'm warm now.

Alex. Levangeline ! it could not have been the evening air.

Lev. Feel my heart now.—Alexander ! for the last

165 three weeks my life has been one long loving thought of thee—for I could say that I have loved and that is all. And when I was away from thee the world seemed gone with thee. Though I have suffered much by absence, and distrust, yet I would not exchange my sorrows

170 for twice the happiness of others, for they were the woes that I endured to conquer gloom, and my present wretchedness, from anxious cares, grows dear to me, since it is suffering for *one* I love.

Alex. Then forget all you have heard.

175 *Lev.* I must know more before I can grant that.

Alex. I will feed thy ears to satiety, if I have but thy

prayers in expiation, for the pain I would occasion thee
in listening to my tale.

Lev. Let me hear the rest, for I was born to gratify
myself, so that I only wronged no one else.   180

Alex. The one in whom you have reason to find a lover,
is the Count Tertsky, who by the request of your god-
father is on his return from the embassy at Constantinople
this very hour.

Lev. Where, and from whom, have you learned this?   185

Alex. From those who are in your father's secret coun-
sel; and though I had it in the first instance as an
insinuation, yet hourly musings has strengthened it into
a fact.

Lev. But surely you are not jealous of Nicholas. You   190
know when I was very young, he was the only one that I
often met, and sought to please me; to humor me in every
little fancy; and thus we often spent hours together, and
really in our childish hearts fancied ourselves as lovers.
Afterwards in my ignorance, and perhaps his own too,   195
we thought indeed we loved, and it may have been rightly
too; for our feelings were different from what the world
calls friendship, and not of the same nature that exists
between sister and brother;—years have gone by since
last we parted, and with them my sensations, and I trust 200
his own.

Alex. You sadly wrong me,—how could you, Levangeline, thus brand me with jealousy—he is as dear to me as
myself.   [*Walks aside, and looks into the sky.*

Lev. (*Humorously.*) Are you an astrologer that you   205
are looking on the stars to decide our fate?

Alex. Pardon me, Levangeline. I was gazing there,
as on an empty space,—I have no thoughts that are not
of you.

Lev. I am called,—I will be with you again, Alexander.   210

Alex. I cannot linger, dearest.

Lev. You would not leave me thus?

Alex. When would you have me with you again?

Lev. (*Takes a flower from her bouquet.*) See this
flower,—it was a favorite with my father, and when he   215
died, my mother planted others like it on his grave. It
is a curious one too, which philosophy has named Mi-

mosa ; but most do vulgarly call the sensitive plant,—
beautifully associated by name to the idea it emblems.
220 Tender, timorous, and pale, it contracts and even closes
beneath the touch ; and if rudely handled dies at once.
Take it, Alexander,—and when it next sleeps, come to me.
    Alex. It contracts already beneath my touch.
    Lev. I knew it would ere I gave it thee.
225   *Alex.* It has a blest meaning, interpreted—you would
have me *never* from you.
    Lev Yes !
    Alex. I promise then, to be enslaved to thee, the four
faces of the dial around. Farewell !   [*Exit*, L.
230   *Lev.* Adieu !   [*Exit by the balcony.*

Scene III.—*A Street.*

Enter Michael, L.

    Mich. (L.) Alas and alack-a-day that brought my
master from the legation at Paris,—for here I am clung
to his lordship as a trail to a falling star,—whichever way
his fancy turns, I must be shifted,—for, like every one
235 in love's service, his thoughts begin with the cock's crow-
ing, and never cease till the cooing of the nightingale,
and his task,—and *my service* much the same. I am to
prepare for a serenade to his lady this night—that is I
am to make the arrangements, and then to see that they
540 are carried out—therefore I must be looking after the
musicians. (*Takes a card from his pocket.*) The house
must be near by, from the direction on the card. (*Music
heard in one of the houses off*, R.) There it is. (*Walks up to
the door*, R., *and knocks. Music ceases, and five Musicians,*
245 *with an attendant enter from the house.*)
    Mus. (C.) Here we are—your will.
    Mich. (*To 1st Mus.*) Pray, my good friend, art thou
akin to the musician of the Grand Opera at Paris, that
charged each flourish of his trumpet, for signalizing the
250 entrance of the army, as a solo ?
    1st Mus. Nay, my good sir.
    Mich. (*To 2d Mus.*) What is your instrument ?
    2d Mus. Mine is the clarionet, sir.

Mich. I like that the most for my purpose,—for it carries the air so well.   What other instruments have we to   255
fill a quintette ?

3d Mus. Mine is the violin,—one that I would not
exchange for a bank.

Mich. (*Humorously.*) That is not for a broken one.

4th and 5th Mus. We play the violin.   260

1st Mus. I perform the part of the violoncello.

Mich. (*To Attendant.*) What is your part ?

Attend. My part, or let me rather say duty, is to carry
the luggage all the week, and like all others that have but
one shirt, to lay a bed all Saturday.   265

Mich. You must have learnt of old,—it is no crime to
be poor.

Attend. No,—no, your honor, else I would have been
born in a prison.   [*All laugh.*

Mich. But you could change your calling.   270

Attend. Pray tell me how ?

Mich. Simply by learning another trade.

Attend. It is very hard to learn old dogs new tricks.

Mich. Well, now, to the object of my errand.   I am
here to arrange for a serenade this night.   275

1st Mus. To whom ?

Mich. To the Countess Manderstem.

1st Mus. Is she as handsome as it is said ?

Mich. I think I might join in common report, and call
her passing fair, though I have never seen her ladyship.   280

1st Mus. You'll not be compromised by that opinion.

Mich. What sum do you name as the terms of our
engagement ?   ·

1st Mus. A sum of florins counted to the twentieth.

Mich. Agreed.   285

Enter ALFRED, *unobserved,* L.

Alf. (*Approaching.*) But there is one part of the bargain you have not touched on.

Mich. (*Anxiously.*) What is that ?

Alf. The price for leaving off. (*Takes* MICHAEL *aside,
and speaks to him apart.*) The Count is ill of a distemper,   290
and your master bade me tell you to put off the serenade.

Mich. (*Aloud.*) Do you hear that—your services for this night are hereby dispensed with.

Attend. I'm glad of that, for I had already felt as the
295 circus rider in facing the balloon.

Alf. That was ?

Attend. He wished he was well through it.

Mich. Well, then, I do not know that I can advise you better, than, for each to return by the way he came, and
300 keep himself in readiness for my next orders.

1st Mus. Let us know your orders in time.
                              [*Musicians exeunt by the house.*

Alf. (*To* MICHAEL.) Let's follow into the house.

Mich. You will oblige them better, by keeping out of it.
                    [*Exeunt* ALFRED *and* MICHAEL, *by the house.*

SCENE IV.—*An ante-chamber in the mansion of the* COUNT
MANDERSTEM ; *table supplied with medicine and a crystal
cup*, L. C.

COUNT MANDERSTEM *discovered seated before a table*, C.,
resting his head on a pillow.   Servant in waiting.

Count. (*Raising his head.*) Ugh ! ugh !
305 *Serv.* (L. C.) Will your lordship have anything ?

Count. Is—is, Levangeline in the house ?

Serv. I think I heard her voice without, the moment that your lordship wakened.

Count. Tell her I would see her.   [*Exit Servant*, L.

Enter LEVANGELINE, L., *followed by the Servant.*

310   *Count.* (*To Servant.*) You may retire to await commands.   [*Exit Servant*, L.

Lev. Were you wanting anything, father ?

Count. No,—I have been dosing till this moment. What is the hour ?
315 *Lev.* Near eight.

Count. (*Aside.*) And he is not yet come to claim her !—
(*aloud.*) I feel chilly about my shoulders,—I thought I heard the cracking of the wood on the hearth, but I don't feel the heat,—cover my shoulders.

Lev. (*Aside.*) He is flighty. (*Aloud.*) It is spring time,   320
close on to Easter.

Count. I must have been dreaming then. My child! I
must have a word with you. Strengthen me with my
tonic.

Lev. (*Handing a glass.*) Drink this, and let me know   325
if it be strong enough.

Count. Ay, it could not be improved. Come be seated
near me. (*Seats herself*, L.) This is what I would tell
you. Your father was a younger branch of a most noble
family, whose deeds of moment that shed lustre on their   330
lives, and brought credit to their country's name, have
long been annalled amongst the 'worthy of our race;—
your mother, I see her, as I often have, most beautifully
by nature pencilled in thy own countenance, could boast
of descent from ancestral names that held places in this   335
world's history quite as meritorious,—whose lives are
likewise written in their country's chronicles. You were
their only child, and were bred in all the care their
enviable and most happy lot could fully offer; you were
just of the age that increasing interest first sets strongly   340
on, and marks her own, when it was your misfortune to
lose your father, in whom I myself was so severely bereft
of a friend, and brother,—I say first a friend, for there
may be a friend still dearer than a brother, but he was
both.   To proceed,—his loss was so severely felt by your   345
dear mother, that she remained for a long time inconsolable,
and though never returning to her former gaiety, that had
made her the peculiar charm to the court and circle she
had ever moved in,—yet, as was thought by all around,
her Ladyship had quite withstood her life's most sore trial,   350
when suddenly she drooped, and died,—just distancing
her lamented Lordship's fate by eighteen months. (*Pauses.*)
That pain again. I have past through in rapid succession
two paroxysms, the bane of this disordered state, as you
have witnessed,—but soon in turn my third may come   355
upon me, and as these are of such a nature when thus
ushered on by such small intervals of time, the fevers
become more obstinate, and life more doubtful,—a feeling
pervades me as though the next would be my last.

Lev. Nay, nay, my father! give not thought to such   360

6

devouring fancies,—think of me! You have been all to
me I could desire,—in you I have had a father,—a pro-
tector,—what would I have been without you?

Count. Levangeline! you are, as ever, my inmost
365   thought.

Enter SERVANT, L.

Serv. A letter for your lordship, and an answer if it be
your pleasure.

Count. (*Handing the letter to* LEVANGELINE.) What
are the contents?

370   *Lev.* (*Breaks the seal, and reads.*) "In accordance with
your Lordship's instructions, and expressed desire, as con-
tained in your favor last received, I have the honor to
inform you, that I have lost no time in making the necessary arrangements for my return; although the legation
375   is at this time much occupied by questions and delibera-
tions of moment. I would further state, that, I am here
in town, to wait upon you at any moment your Lordship
may be pleased to command me. In haste, but most
sincerely and obediently,   ·   DE TERTSKY."

[*On perceiving the signature she exhibits signs of the
deepest emotions, unobserved by the* COUNT. JOSEPHINE
has entered during the reading of the communication.

380   *Count.* I would have you follow my dictation—hastily
make my due acknowledgments,—and further state it
to be my pleasure to receive his Lordship at the earliest
possible moment.

[LEVANGELINE *motions in dumb show with* JOSEPHINE,
*who writes, seals the note, and with it follows her in con-
versation to the door.*

Count. Command the presence of a servant.

[LEVANGELINE *rings the bell.*

Enter SERVANT, L.

385   *Serv.* Your Lorship's commands?

Count. Immediately go and inform Frederick to come,—

say to Alexander, *I'm dying*, leave word with Francis, in case he should have remained in town till this hour, to come and be with me in my last moments.

[Exit SERVANT, L.

Enter ALEXANDER *and* NICHOLAS, C. D.

[ALEXANDER *and* NICHOLAS *take the hand of the* COUNT, *and gaze upon* LEVANGELINE *with a look of hesitation as whether to speak, when she starts up from her knees, on which she has remained in a state of mental stupefaction, and collecting herself converses with* NICHOLAS *apart for a moment.*

Count. Most too late. (*They seat themselves,* L.) closer,   390
closer, while I speak of what I have brought you from a distance, and what concerns each of you. Levangeline, I've already told you of your father and mother, when I paused from weakness,—in your mother's last moments she sent for me, as I have for you, and impressed upon   395
me a duty to fulfill,—the last that remains unperformed of your father's testimony. It is this,—as a mark of his friendship for the Count Tertsky's regards for his only child, Levangeline, and in deference to what he looked upon as a mutual tenderness on their part from childhood,   400
he thereby offered him her hand whenever his lordship should desire to ask it. He, a dying man, made this request of me, and I have called you from afar to——
that pain again!

Count. Allow me to recover strength for my next   405
encounter.   [LEVANGELINE *arranges his pillow.*

Enter FREDERICK *and* FRANCIS, C. D.

Fran. (L. C.) Your servant instructed us to be with your Lordship immediately, as we were passing the mansion.

Count. And so I did, for I thought that I was dying,   410
and would have had you with me. But I am happy again in my strength. You, too, are happy, Francis :—you are entering life amid friends beloved, and academic laurels.

And Frederick, you remember how I have counselled
415 with you! Levangeline! where are your hands that have
so often pressed my forehead? You have not left me!
Levangeline!

    Lev. What is your pleasure, father?

    Count. (*After some exertion.*) Come nearer, and give
420 me your hand;—and Nicholas, yours. (*To* LEVANGELINE.)
Receive this, as one whom your father deemed fit to be
your husband, and his son. This day be happy both, and
may to-morrow's Sun, shine down to grace your nuptials.

[LEVANGELINE *sinks into* ALEXANDER'S *arms.* FREDERICK
    rests the COUNT'S *head.* NICHOLAS *rests his head on his*
    hand.

END OF ACT II.

ACT III.

SCENE I.—*A drawing room in the mansion of the* COUNT
MANDERSTEM; *a transparent door,* C.

Enter LEVANGELINE, L.

LEVANGELINE. (L. C.)

'M all estranged since yesternoon. So
many strange goings on have happened
since then, that I believe all things
possible 'twixt now and the morrow.
Something of earthly bliss have I en-   5
joyed, but now it seems to me, the Sun
is setting on my fate; and what's to follow I'm
ignorant of.

Enter ALEXANDER.

Alex. (*Entering from* L.) Levangeline!
Lev. Alexander! (*Aside.*) Hope has not proved deceit-   10
ful;—(*Aloud.*) yet, there's a melancholy thought that is
striving to shun the light, which I see lurking beneath
that sadness in thy countenance.
Alex. (*Aside.*) It has been the midnight's study with
me to determine how I can speak the last farewell,—to   15
tell her, we must part. I could one death endure, but
how the death that is comprised in that one word depart;—
death is but the temporary separation of the soul and
body, but *this parting* is more than that,—it is the death
of love, the ultimate separation of one's soul's far better   20
part!
Lev. Come, be seated. (*They seat themselves,* R.) What
has detained you till this hour?
Alex. I cannot tell.
Lev. You are then possessed of a mystery, and are for-   25
bidden by the dictates of your conscience to unfold it.

Alex. Levangeline! no woman can truly love the man that she suspects.

Lev. It was not thus you talked, when we parted last
30   in the garden.   At the midnight of that day I blessed
thee on my knees, for I looked on thee and sincerely believed thee my friend and lover.   Oh ! the wages of folly
that fall on me now,—a blindfold and credulous mistaken
soul ! Should not thy voice falter to express thy thoughts,
35   and thy very countenance blush when thou recallest how
you gently tied me within thy arms, and with a fond en-
dearment, and gentle touch, that made all nature smile
upon our love, as when first thou fixedst upon my finger,—
This cherished memento of thy faith's vow :
40   " A ring fashioned as a serpent coiléd,
Most ancient emblem of eternity.
The diamond, say a token of our true
Love's eternal purity ;"—which I have
Sworn, that I will grasp ev'n in my death's pang !
45   *Alex.* Levangeline ! I well knew that I was dear to thee,
I saw it in the first animated glance that you cast upon
me,—those flowers you gave me as an assurance of your
first and only love I kept a vigil eye upon for half this
day, and though fast fading do yet remain to witness thy
50   own love and pledge of faith.

Lev. Pray proceed.

Alex. This very morn I woke from a dream with the
words of Ossian on my mind.   Have you ever read that
author ?
55   *Lev.* Not since I left the convent, and my recollection
of his writings has grown very faint.

Alex. I will then remind you of the passage,—it occurs
in the description where Ossian deplores the loss of
Malvina.   It is this :—" Bend thy blue course, O stream !
60   round the narrow plain of Lutha.*   Let the green woods
hang over it, from their hills : the sun look on it at noon.
The thistle is there on its rock, and shakes its beard to
the wind.   The flower hangs its heavy head, waving, at
times, to the gale.   'Why dost thou awake me, O gale ?'
65   it seems to say.   'I am covered with the drops of heaven !
The time of my fading is near, the blast that shall scatter

* Lutha, *swift stream.*

my leaves. To-morrow shall the traveller come ; he that
saw me in my beauty shall come ; his eyes will search
the field, but they will not find me !' " *

Lev. Alexander ! (*He throws himself at her feet, seizes*   70
her hands, and covers his forehead with them.) Our parting would be to me only a changed name for death, and
though you do not know what grief would do with me,
I'll tell you—my life would not long remain.

Alex. How would you have me act—you have learned   75
that there is another who has a prior claim to your endear-
ment ; a seal that has long been promised with your own
father's blessing. You know that the sacred bond of friendship binds me to him as strongly as the cord of love
between ourselves ; I have concluded that one of us three   80
must make the sacrifice,—*it shall be me.*

Lev. I ask it of you as a favor, that you will not go on
further in this manner,—I ask it in the name of the love
you bear for my peace and tranquillity.

Enter IDA, R.

Ida. The Count Tertsky awaits your pleasure.   85

Lev. Tell him I am now engaged—that I cannot see
him this moment—that I will meet him presently.

               [*Exit* IDA, R.

I feel in such a condition that I scarce know the meaning of the words I uttered. Will you not linger, and   90
let us receive him together.

Alex. I cannot.

Lev. Then say adieu,—and of this be assured that the
joy of our next meeting will repay the pangs that this has
occasioned.   95

Alex. I cannot say so.

Lev. Thou would'st not leave me to despairing hope !—
Look on me—heart and soul I am thine own—since I
have known thee I have been thine, and only thine.
Thou know'st I am and have been but thine only. Dost   100
thou not hear me ? Have I done nothing, suffered,

---

* *Cf.*, the Elegy on the death of Malvina, the daughter of Tos-
can in Ossian's poem of Berrathon ; translated by James Macpher-
son, Esq.

and abandoned nothing for thee, since I have known thee ?
Why was it so ill-fated that we should meet,—or else
should I never have been plunged into this wretchedness !
105 But now, methinks, though thou should'st hate me, still am
I thine ! Though thou should'st leave me ! no—no, thou
could'st not do so base a thing as leave me—could'st thou ?
    Alex. I could for ever listen, but——
    Lev. Alexander ! remember, thou mayst deny me, but
110 I shall be as ever, true to thee, sole possessor of this heart,
as life and thought will witness, while they remain within
me.   And though death should steal on me, and reason
itself should leave me, thy own dear name would be the
last upon my lisping breath !
115   *Alex.* Ah, dearest ! would that thy faith from on high,
was crowned with blessings endless as thy love. (*Aside,
after a pause.*) While thou art standing near me, sorrow
seems but something without a being, but in thy absence
shall I soon-learn its meaning. (*Aloud.*) Adieu !
120   *Lev.* Adieu ! (*Exit,* ALEXANDER, R.) Adieu !—adieu !—
(*Throws herself into a chair,* R.) Though I am crossed by
many forethoughts, still can I no wrong ever conceive of
thee.

Enter IDA, C. D.

Ida. (C.) Count Tertsky awaits.   [*Exit,* R.

Enter NICHOLAS, C. D., *dressed as a huntsman.*

125   *Lev.* (*With a courtsey.*) Nicholas !
    Nich. (R. C.) Levangeline !
    Lev. (*Approaching.*) We were not so distant when we
met of old ;—you are not looking the same as on your
return yesterday :—are you well ?
130   *Nich.* I am in body. (*Aside.*) If but my heart was as
the sage of old would have had the breast of man,
a mirror in which we could view each the other's faults,
and learn our feelings !—I must say something. (*Aloud.*)
We are nine years older, and the remembrance of our
135 former love, say friendship if you choose, has returned to
us amidst sorrowful trials and disasters.

Lev. True it is silent grief that gnaws the deepest; it is your consolation for the loss you may meet at an early day in one, that has been bound to you by the strongest cords of friendship; and to whom I was as dear as his   140
only child.

Nich. (*Aside.*) If I go on thus, I shall never have the fortitude to gain the object of my visit.—I must change her thoughts.—Tell me wherefore looks Frederick so altered ?   145

Lev. A cloister in a far distant convent would tell the tale of one coarsely attired, but well pleased to calmly endure religious hardships, to fast and next to chill at midnight prayers, to live with melancholy, half speechless souls like herself, and bless kind heaven that her days are   150
lengthened to expiate her grief occasioned by one she loved.

Nich. As has often happened.   But the cause——

Lev. Was this; while he was mistrusting the faithfulness of the tenderness that had taken possession of the   155
heart of one towards him, he became attracted by another.

Enter IDA, *hurriedly,* R.

Ida. (c.)   A letter for my lady.   Excuse my rude interruption, but the bearer bade me lose not the earliest opportunity to give it to you.   [*Exit,* R.

Lev. Who can have such an urgent call on my atten-   160
tion ? (*Observes the address.*) It is Alexander's writing ! (*Is about to break the seal, when* NICHOLAS *interferes.*)

Nich. I pray you, Levangeline, not to break the seal in my presence.

Lev. You must be acquainted with its contents, or something connected with its history.   I am warned of   165
something wrong in your hesitation and silence.

Nich. Levangeline ! have I ever deceived you thus far in my life ?

Lev. No—no !

Nich. I have not learned its contents, but—but—   170
(*aside*) the truth would kill her; (*aloud*) it is a lasting proof of his *love* for *you,*—his *friendship* for *me.*

7

Lev. This contention between hope and fear has made me frantic.

175   *Nich.* Levangeline ! by that confidence you place in me, I again pray you to so far respect my feelings as not to open it in my presence.

Lev. Here then let it rest, within my breast I'll keep it, and read it quietly to myself alone.

180   *Nich.* (*Goes up to window.*) This beauteous evening is such an one as that on which we used to pass upon the waters, caring for and seeing nought but ourselves ; those long, gentle moonlights, when my fond guitar and thy sweet voice went up to Heaven in softest melody. It is

185 gone !

Lev. Oh, Nicholas, speak not of it ! There are incidents in this world, which to look back and to dwell on, only occasion the most painful sensations to our present life. Let us enjoy the present and forget the past.

190   *Nich.* Levangeline, it is in keeping with those sentiments which you have just expressed, that I would speak. You were my first love,—and shall be my last. Mine was a passion that like a seedling planted in the peasant's early life, who goes afar, and returns in hope of finding

195 his seed grown to a tree, with swelling trunk, and spreading leaves, but——

Lev. (*Interrupting.*) Spare me ! I know I am thy rightfully affianced bride, but——

Nich. Levangeline ! what passed between your father

200 and the Count, save what thou hast heard thyself, I am a stranger to. That thy father should have deemed me a fit suitor for thy hand, was just, and I am grateful to his memory, but true love looks to one alone for its sanctioning,—its chosen subject.

205   *Lev.* Thou meanest,——

Nich. That *he* would have blown the bud open too suddenly,—genial warmth and dew alone can by degrees effect its unfolding, and cause it to open its heart, and give forth its perfume, for if suddenly opened it will fade

210 away before the morrow, leaving nothing of its perfume behind. Levangeline ! I can never receive such a gift—love desires freedom, and constraint or even that which bears

its appearance causes discontent, and debases the nobler
heart of man and woman.

Lev. I listen—let me hear more.   215

Nich. But it is to another end that I would speak, Levangeline. I know your heart, and the one to whom
you have already given it, and rather than he should
sacrifice life, name, ambition's hopes for me—in the
name of the friendship I bear him, in the name of your   220
love for him I have resolved to make a sacrifice for both.

Lev. Oh! no—no.   [*Looking fondly on him.*

Nich. It is not despair that drives me to it, but the
conviction that I have filled up the measure of my life;
that I have reached the day on which I must sacrifice   225
myself to the love you bear him. Why should I not confess it? One of us three must do it—it shall be me.

Lev. Listen, listen, to reason's voice,—let me entreat
you to be more calm, and hear me!

Nich. Speak then.   230

Lev. Be yourself again, and overcome an unfortunate
attachment to me, whose only lot is to pity you. Why
must it be only me—me, who has sworn, by a purity that
equals love itself, to belong to another!

Nich. (*Who has been pacing the stage; stops suddenly,
and interrupting* LEVANGELINE.) Reason on the subject   235
as you may, combine all the arguments which you can
propose as an inducement for me to desist from my intentions, and you will not have in the least affected my
determinations.

Lev. Grant me but a moment's patience, and listen   240
further;—you are deceiving yourself,—you are seeking
not only your own destruction, but my sorrow, and what
more I dare not tell. Is it not only the impossibility of
possessing me, that makes the desire the stronger? Seek,
and you will certainly find in this world, another woman   245
whose love remains unpledged, and who has the power,
and would wish to make you happy. Look for such a
woman, and be persuaded of it, that you will certainly
find her. I have passed a dreadful day of apprehension
for each of us,—the peculiar conditions that bind us   250
mutually together only strengthen it. Seek from
another quarter a woman worthy of your tenderness,—

come back,—and let us together enjoy the happiness to
the fullest degree that can spring from the most perfect
255 friendship that exists! Do as I have spoken. Come
again soon,—but not before to-morrow, for I will send for
Alexander yet to-day.   [*Gems-horn heard faintly.*

    Nich. I will reflect, Levangeline. I must now be away,
for the huntsmen were already collecting when I entered:
260 and I promised to join in the chase.

Enter IDA, R.

    Ida. There is a messenger without that craves to give
a communication to the Count Tertsky.

    Lev. Ask him to come here.   [*Exit,* R.

Enter MESSENGER, R.

    Mess. I beg your lordship's pardon, and my lady's.
265 This is the Count de Tertsky.

    Nich. I am.

    Mess. (*Handing a note.*) This is a note addressed to
your lordship.

    Nich. How came you acquainted of my presence here?
270   *Mess.* I was directed to wait with it on the grounds,
and to deliver it into no one's hands but your lordship's.
I did so, but learning that your lordship had not arrived
at the hunting lodge, and was most probably at the mansion,—since your lordship had been seen some time since
275 entering the doors,—I thought it would be most advisable
for me to lose no time in enquiring as I have done.

    Nich. You were quite right. You may retire. (*Exit
Messenger,* R.) *It is Alexander's writing.*—(*Opens it with
hesitation.*) I cannot read it.

    Lev. Read,—read—let me know the worst, though it
280 should prove poison's own draught.

    Nich. Then I will read. (*Reads.*) " My dear Tertsky:—
the morning of that day (to-morrow) on which you have
invited me to the hunt, at the very hour when we had
destined to depart, cold mother nature may hold all that
285 is mortal of this agitated, broken, but once happy man,
who in his last hours of life knows no pleasure so great

as that of being loved by one, with whose welfare we are
so intimately connected. (*He pauses, and then resumes
in irregular accents.*) Since you left me I have passed a
dreadful hour, or rather let me say a propitious one ; for   290
it has fixed my purpose ;—*I am resolved to die!* When
I tore myself from her this very hour, my senses were in
the utmost tumult and disorder, my heart beat heavy,
hope and every ray of pleasure were fled from me for ever,
and destruction seemed to encompass my very being.   295
My troubled soul has been tossed to and fro by many
ideas, and as many schemes ! at length I have resolved on
one thought which is fixed firmly on my mind,—I will
die—a sacrifice for *you.*"

   Lev. (*Who has been listening to the letter, with visible
signs of the deepest agitation, slowly advances, and throws
herself into his arms.*) Oh !   300

   Nich. What would you have me do ?

   Lev. What can you !

   Nich. I will tell you. (LEVANGELINE *withdraws from
him.—Aside.*) This is the last and worst struggle of all.
What hearts I have to contend with !—(*Aloud,*) Fear   305
nothing.—I would not rob him of a holier love than mine.
I will depart !

   Lev. Depart ?

   Nich. (*Endeavoring to evade his meaning.*) That is, I
will away, seek for him, and find him. He may be ap-   310
proaching here this very moment, and it would be best
for us not to meet in this condition—it would only serve
to fix his resolution the deeper. It is best for you to
meet him alone. I shall return, and will be at the hunting lodge. You can send for me there, if you should wish   315
to see me. How—how should I ever lose such a friend
as that ! If he comes, you will endeavor to calm him,
and use your best efforts to assuage him from his deter-
mination. We may yet all be happy,—happy as we have
always been since our childhood ! I have nothing to ask   320
your pardon, since first we met ; have I ?

   Lev. Oh, no !

   Nich. Do you remember when last we parted ? I came
one evening, and saw you weeping by my side,—I kissed
you, and put that cross upon your neck, the same as that   325

you wear ; and its brilliants aided by the gentle light of dawn —I remember well the tint, I've seen it often in the East—seemed to cast upon your face a ray of hope ;—the great cathedral bell tolled out for Easter morn's mass, we

330 bade farewell,—you went afar to an Italian convent, where you remained till I departed for the East. You counted scarcely twelve years when last I saw your face ; we would still have recognized ourselves, would'st thou not, Levangeline ?

335   *Lev.* Ah yes, ah yes !—I only cared to be mistress of this cross, for it was of the few things that I loved half-killingly.

     Nich. Have you ever opened the clasp that closes its back ?

340   *Lev.* I never have. (*She opens it with the aid of* NICH-OLAS, *and takes out a folded paper, which he opens and presents her to read.*) "Love, you will not now understand these words written in that most beautiful of all languages ; but at an early day, when you shall have

345 arrived in that land, you will find those that may introduce you to their sense. Be careful in whom you confide, for fear of being compromised."

     Nich. Read the lines in Italian.

     Lev. I cannot but to myself alone.

350   *Nich.* Then I will save you that pain ; and when soon you shall think how fondly hope has risen on you, and one shall take you as the pledge of future fortune,— remember the past:—but do not grieve over me, when you shall soon learn how I have loved you both.

355   *Lev.* Adieu !

     Nich. Farewell ! (*Aside.*) it may be *forever.*—(*Aloud.*) Think of me sometimes whilst distance divides us, but it never shall unless you wish, if spirits think and are empowered to look on the world beneath, for you ever

360 shall be my first and only thought.

[*He draws close to her, their eyes meet, she stands silent for a moment, and then perceiving for the first time the firmness of his resolution, throws herself into his arms ; he presses her to his heart. Door alarum heard without,* c.

Nich. Hark, what's that noise ? 'tis the alarum !

[ALEXANDER *is observed at* c. d., *as in the act of entering, but pauses, and intently gazes on* NICHOLAS *and* LEVANGELINE *unobserved by either.*

Lev. Heavens ! let's be gone ! if *he* should be come !
   [*They part from their embrace.* NICHOLAS *exits,* R.
Lev. Oh, Nicholas ! till this unpropitious moment, I
never knew, how dear I was to thine memory:—but in   365
these unaccountable issues, my senses seem dissolved,
and my only solace seems to be destruction.

[*As* LEVANGELINE *approaches* c. d., *she beholds* ALEXANDER, *and shrieks. He enters just in time to catch her in his arms in the act of fainting.*

END OF ACT III.

ACT IV.

SCENE I.—*A woody place adjoining the grounds attached to* COUNT MANDERSTEM'S *Mansion ; a view of mountains in the distance ; across the stage back runs a practicable winding rocky pass ;* Hunter's Lodge, R. 1. E., *stake, spit and other arrangements for a roast,* R. C. *front.*

MICHAEL, (*Entering from* L.)

 IDN'T know that it was of any use,—scratched on it,—and burnt it for waste paper.

Enter IDA, *from Lodge,* R. 1. E., *with a bouquet of yellow roses in her hand.*

5   *Ida.* Good day to you, Monsieur Michael—how passes the day with you ?
Mich. Ask of my note.
Ida. Where is it ?
Mich. Ask of master's coachman's daughter,—ask of the fire.
10   *Ida.* It's not burnt ?
Mich. She did not know that it was of any use,—scratched on it, and burnt it for waste paper.
Ida. Of what did it speak ?
Mich Of woeful absence from thee, to be sure, for the
15   last twelve hours.
Ida. Truly ?
Mich. As you are an angel.
Ida. Not a fallen one, from whom you have any harm to look for ?
20   *Mich.* Nay, nay, an archangel.
Ida. (*Observing for the first time the difference in the color of his stockings.*) Oh, my !
Mich. What's that ?

Ida. Oh, you'll kill me with laughter !
Mich. You don't understand me !
Ida. Did eyes ever behold the like !   25
Mich. The like !—why I was handsome yesterday !
Ida. Oh, Michael, do look at your stockings !
Mich. Yes—I've lost another stocking—
Ida. How,—not by that dog again ?
Mich. This time, it blew off the clothes' line, and   30
master's coachman's daughter lost all sight of it.   Those
stockings, the only relic that my grand sire left when he
was forced to leave his native France, on the revocation
of the edict of Nantes.
Ida. But still you have got one pair remaining.   35
Mich. But how ?
Ida. Why the dog tore one hose of the first pair,—and
the wind took one of the second pair, and still there's two
remaining.
Mich. Yes, but they are each of a different color : and   40
apropros, let me tell you another morning's incident—
Ida. This daughter of your master's coachman must
have some designs on you.
Mich. Believe me, you have no need to fear jealousy
now : but when I was first seated at the table, where she   45
sat at my right hand, I could not help observing that her
eye was constantly and steadily fixed on me.   It was not
for me to take notice of it at first, judging, as any one
would, that it was due to the attractive power of my personal charms, and that time would induce her to some   50
bolder device.   But finding that my face was still the
object to which her eyes were directed, I began to grow
much abashed at my own modesty, when, to my sorrowful satisfaction, master informed me, that the eye which
I thought had been so steadily fixed on me, and excited   55
my vanity, was only a *glass eye,* and was as unmeaning
in its look by day, as it was quiet at night, when it rested
on her toilet table, by the side of her glass.
Ida. From high expectations often comes lofty tum-
bling.   60
Mich. (*Kneeling and taking her hand.*) As lowly as I
am now :—the sight of those yellow roses has made me feel
years younger, for since I have seen them in your hand
                                          8

these five minutes, I have become in love with a woman,
65 who, if she be still alive must be five years within my own
age.

Ida. Then you have—have *loved before ?*

Mich. Let me tell you the story—it is the remembrance
of which, just refreshed by the sight of that rose, that,
70 even now, does not fail to agitate me to an extreme
degree. I was twenty years of age ; that was thirty
years ago, when my uncle announced to me one morning,
that he had determined on placing me in the army, in a
regiment that had been raised in our village. I must
75 confess to my being greatly shocked at this,—not that I
had any distaste to a military life, for I should have
wished to have seen nothing more to my taste, than to
find myself in a uniform, surrounded by the roll of the
drum—but I was in love ! nor, indeed, did I venture to
80 speak a word of this to uncle, for I well knew, as there
was an old faction between the families, he would have
urged my enlistment, if for no other reason than to
thwart my attaining the thought of my days and nights.
But I fixed on another plan. I had another uncle of
85 nearly the same age as I am at this time, who had much
fondness for young folk, and had the good sense to be
never better pleased than when he was the occasion of
pleasing others—he made himself the confidant and pro-
tector of all the youth of the neighborhood,—assisted
90 every worthy applicant in cases of debt———

Ida. (Interrupting.) But what did he do in your case ?

Mich. As I was soon a going to say,—I went to his
house, and said to him,—Dear uncle, I have fallen into a
misfortune. "You don't know what that means," said
95 he. Don't joke, uncle. "I will bet you, that you have
met with no misfortune." Now, uncle, I have too much
consideration to be the occasion of your losing, which
you most undoubtedly would. "Well, tell me, then,
what has befell you ?" Uncle Joseph has told me, that,
100 he has decided that I shall enlist. "There's no misfortune
in that,—for setting aside the risk of life, you have always
promotion in view." Yes, always in view, answered I.
"Are you wanting in courage ?" Oh ! no. "Well, then, I
can't understand that you have any reason for not wishing

to be a soldier." The reason is—that—that—I wish to 105
be married. "Bah!" That is no consolation for one in
love! "I should like to be in love myself, once more,
up to my neck.—But, tell me, who this girl may be?"
Uncle, she is an angel! "Oh! yes, I don't doubt but she
is an archangel—but what earthly name does she answer 110
to?" Her name is Ida. "That is her christian name, I
want to know her family name." I hesitated at this,—
knowing that there had been years ago, a faction between
the families—I nevertheless answered his demand by tell-
ing him her name is Ida Amelot.   115

Ida. (*Aside.*) 'Tis strange—Ida Amelot—but then my
lover's name was Michael Bonasse,—not Michael Cabalé.

Mich. And I continued, without leaving uncle time for
chiding me, that for all her name is Amelot, she has a
mind and heart! "Ah, yes! I don't doubt but you think 120
so—and if our family used to have sad wranglings, it is
no reason that the effect of the evil should descend like an
heirloom to our children. But is your affection paid in
return, as we used to say?" Really, uncle, that is just
what I wish to learn; for I do not know that she even 125
suspects me of loving her. "You know very little of the
sex, to know so little—she knew it as soon as yourself,"
said he. "Well," he continued, "there are some chances
against her being yours. You know of the family dissen-
sions, and I doubt if your uncle will bestow his nephew 130
upon her." Well then, uncle, there's only one course for
me to choose. "Nonsense!" said he, "don't commit any
folly, but follow my course." Very well, uncle. "In
the first place you cannot marry at eighteen," he continued. Why not? "Because I won't allow you, and if 135
you cross my admonitions you will lose my aid, and this
marriage will never take place at all." He continued—
"now, if the girl loves you, and should be willing to wait
three years for you—" *Three years!* said I. Uncle
reassured me, "if I began to argue about it, he would desist 140
from lending me any aid whatever," at the same time
declaring, as before, that "without his aid the marriage
would never take place. If she will wait," he went on,
"you can join a regiment, and thus fulfil your uncle
Joseph's wishes. But not at Cherbourg! I will contrive 145

to have you put in one a few leagues from .town, where
you can return at times." Well, uncle, the only question is, if she loves me—how am I to find this out?
" Why simply, by asking her." I dare not—I have often
150 wished to tell her that I loved her, when I have been
abashed at my own timidity, though I have tried to
obtain courage in all ways; I have even written notes
avowing my intentions, and burnt them undelivered;
and when an opportunity offered for speaking to her on
155 the point, the first word always choked me—and I ab-
ruptly changed my talk to some other subject—it is
always the first word that is the difficulty. Dear uncle,
a sudden idea strikes me. "What is it?" I have
determined to write to her. "Do so." I returned home,
160 and sat about writing my note at once. There was no
difficulty in the writing, but it was the delivery of the
note that was to be planned. I lost no time, however,
in fixing upon the means of its delivery to her: I pro-
cured a bouquet of yellow roses, loosened the string, and
165 placed the billetdoux in the middle of the bouquet, and
tied it up again.

Ida. Of what did it tell?

Mich. Of the avowal of my love, and of the desire to
have her acknowledged return, that she would wait for
170 me till such time as I asked her, if she listened to my
entreaties, to wear in her bosom, on that evening, one of
my yellow roses, which I would take as a signal to speak
with her, and I would tell her all that would be necessary
for her to do to secure *our* happiness.

175 *Ida.* (*Aside.*) I become bewildered—what! did you
place a billet within the bouquet?

Mich. Yes.

Ida. And what followed?

Mich. In the evening Ida did not wear a yellow rose
180 in her hair. I was frantic. I told it to my uncle, who
declared, that, "I had been deceived from the first, that
she had never loved me." To which I added, that she
had always acted as though she did,—she always looked
so mild, and seemed so glad whenever she met me, and
185 gently reproached me when I came a little late. " Ah,
women are but women, and love to affect love, for the

sake of having it," said uncle. In this condition, I will-
ingly consented to be mustered in the service for three
years, in the hopes of my being able to forget my Ida,
but it was of no use—at the end of the three years I   190
returned to my uncle's house, and found that she had
even left the country. And, do you believe, that I still
at times think of her, not as she must now appear after
twenty years, but as the youthful dame of seventeen,
with her beautiful brown hair, and, as I used to call them,   195
velvety black eyes.

Ida. Did you never learn what became of Ida Amelot?

Mich. Only this much—that she became the wife of
one of your countrymen, whom she met in France, and
settled in his country.   200

Ida. But your name has not always been Michael
Cabalé?

Mich. No; that is the name I adopted while under my
Uncle's roof. My father's name was Michael Bonasse.

Ida. Is it possible!—*Michael!*   205

Mich. What means this?

Ida. Yes, *she loved you!*

Mich. She—who—who told you so! But what of the
yellow roses?

Ida. She never saw the billet.   210

Mich. (*Aside.*) What is the meaning of this—there's
witchcraft at work.

Ida. Your sudden departure threw her into such a condition that her life was for a time despaired of; but in
course of time, like you, she married Stralenheim—and is   215
now a widow.

Mich. Stralenheim!

Ida. Yes, whose widow *I* am.

Mich. What, are you!—you!—Ida Stralenheim?

Ida. As sure as you are Michael Cabalé, and once were   220
Michael Bonasse.

Mich. And the day has come when we should have met,
and loved afresh, without recognizing each other!

Ida. Yes, strange as it appears.

, *Mich.* But tell me something of the bouquet of yellow   225
roses.

Ida. The bouquet—I have always preserved it in a drawer of my bureau, though it has years since faded.

Mich. Bring it out—bring it out. (IDA *exits hastily into the house, and re-enters with the bouquet in her hand.*)

230 Untie it—untie it. (*She unties the bouquet, apparently with much emotion; when the billet falls out; both remain for a while silent.*)

Ida. Will you see me again to-day—at *another* hour

Mich. I understand you, Ida. You are right. It is best that this renewal of our hearts in youth should not effect an event, which is to afford us happiness for the rest

235 of our lives, and thus at least atone for the misfortunes of the past. Who are these nearing?

Ida. The band of monks belonging to the monastery that lies on the mountain yonder.

[MICHAEL *and* IDA *walk up the stage,* R. C.

[*A band of Monks and Choristers passes over the stage, from* R. *to* C., *and enters the rocky pass; goes over to* L., *and exits,* R; *the Choristers singing the following refrain of a chant:*

Give ear, ye blessed above, give ear,
Harken to our ev'ning prayer,
Harken to our fear of despair,
And with success our efforts cheer.

Mich. You tell me that the monastery lies beyond on
240 the mountains?

Ida. Yes:—many is the huntsman that could tell of the hospitable treatment he has met with at the hands of these monks, when he has been compelled to seek shelter over night, under their roof.

[*Exeunt* MICHAEL *and* IDA, L.

[*The inarticulate refrain of a hunting chorus is heard in the distance, off* R.

Hilloa ho! hilloa ho!
The mountains are echoing with hilloa ho!
Up through the woodlands, down through the dale,
Our gemshorns sounding inspire the gale,
And echo, mocking the hunter's tale,
Resounds hilloa! hilloa!

[*At the conclusion of the refrain,* PHILIP *enters from the lodge, stands at the door, and sounds a strain on the gemshorn, which is reflected in an echo, and exits through the door of the lodge. The same inarticulate echo of the refrain is again heard, and dies away as though the party had reached that part of the mountain pass which destroys the echo. A hunting party, headed by* JOHN *and* HENRY, *bearing their prey, enter* R., *on to the rocky pass, and cross over the stage to* L, *and then over to* R., *and to* C., *on to the stage, singing the foregoing refrain.* PHILIP *and his party enter from the lodge, followed by their wives and children, leading a chamois. Other women and children enter from* L. 1 *and* 2 E. *All the characters take up the chorus. Some bring forward a chamois from the lodge, which they arrange on the spit; while others bring forward a dog, which they place in the turnspit. The moon rises, and all the characters join in a waltz.*

SCENE II.—*An Ante-chamber in the mansion of* COUNT MANDERSTEM.

Enter LEVANGELINE, L.

Lev. (L. C.) Not all the morn, not all the live long   245
    morn,
Hast thou been with me !—yet a feeling sense,
Within this breast speaks out,—thou think'st of me !
And that is at least a consolation,
Though it be aught else vain and profitless.   250
                [*Crosses,* R.
Thus am I granted, as in a cloister closed,
Pressed by the weight of sadness and of love,
To ask forgetful dullness stealing on me,
To soften and assuage this gnawing pain from secret
Dwelling on my melancholy thoughts;   255
When waking as from a watchful slumber,
On every side I turn my anxious eyes,
To look for hope, and find that one hope lost.
And though I wander through these lofty halls,

260   Or pace the balconade with longing eyes,
      Nought can I fix my watchful eyes upon,
      But his dear image constanly appears,
      And I become thus savage and forlorn.

    [Crosses to L., and seats herself, resting her head on her
      hand ; and directing her eyes to that part of the wall,
      where she discovers a spider's nest.

      Oh that I were but a child of nature,
265   To admire as an infinitely curious
      Thing, you creature upon the wall,
      Which moves this way and that its jointed limbs,
      And by the sole powers of nature's instinct,
      Guides aright each nicely balanced motion
270   Of its frail frame to pleasurable ends,
      A moment to distract my unstable mind
      From its dark foreboding of forlorn hope !
      I have tried all : yet vainly—vainly tried.—
      The very luxury spread 'neath my feet,
275   And air that floats heavy with fresh'ning sweets,
      Seem but a something wearily loathsome.

    [LEVANGELINE pauses for a moment as in hesitation ;
      then exits, R. ; Re-enters with FRANCIS, C.

    Lev. (R. C.) Do tell me something of Nicholas.
    Fran. Are you prepared for the worst, Levangeline ?
    Lev. (*Gazes on him for a moment, with a countenance*
    expressive of amazement.) Yes.
280   *Fran.* He was scaling a mountain with others, in hot
    pursuit of a chamois that had just fell on his view, when
    from behind a stone, with peerless speed, the animal
    rushed forth, and became entrapped in a bush by his
    crooked horns, that stood high upon his head. In that
285   position it remained till Nicholas quite neared to it,
    when as by love of life, it struggled by a despairing leap
    to extricate itself from among the twigs, when Nicholas
    renewed the pursuit leap after leap, till stepping on a
    stone that chanced to be loosened from the rock, he fell
290   a distance of several yards, and when we reached the

spot, we found him senseless, and in this condition we
bore him to the monastery, intent that he should be made
a subject of all faithful care.

Lev. Is he seriously injured?

Fran. It is the belief that he is not, and that by a   295
proper subsequent course he may quite recover.

Lev. But what of Alexander?—why do you turn
aside from me? (FRANCIS *and* LEVANGELINE *rise.*)   Tell
me—tell me, Francis!

Fran. I am told——   300

Lev. What are you told?

Fran. That Alexander——is——

Lev. Is what?—do not keep me in such dread sus-
pension.

Fran. That he is in a severe state of fever, from which   305
his physicians say, his recovery is doubtful.

[LEVANGELINE, *as soon as she hears this, shrieks, and
swoons in the arms of* FRANCIS.

END OF ACT IV.

ACT V.

SCENE I.—LEVANGELINE'S *bed chamber; a large window extending to the floor, closed by inside shutters, and Italian sash in side flat,* R. 1. E. *Door communicating with the hall, in* R. C. *flat. Two windows, darkened by curtains, in* L. *flat. At the back,* L. C., *a bedstead, with drawn curtains. Bureau* R., *near window. Couch down stage,* L. C. *Small table with a goblet of water, a crystal cup, and different phials on it,* R., *near window.*

As the curtain rises Cathedral chimes faintly heard off R. LEVANGELINE *discovered asleep on the couch,* L. C.; IDA *seated by the window,* L., *has fallen asleep.*

LEVANGELINE, (*Awakening as from a dream.*)

HOU art then saved, and return-ed to me. (*Holds out her arms, as if in the act of embracing some object.*) What shall now part us? (*Suddenly awaking and collecting her thoughts.*) It is but a dream—a dream at last! All has been but a succession of empty images, and I awake to dispel the charm. (*Calls faintly.*) Ida—Ida!

Ida. (*Awaking and coming over,* L.) What would the Countess?

Lev. Poor creature, you were sleeping too;—I thought
15   you looked fatigued when you assisted me from yonder bed to this couch.

Ida. I pray pardon of my lady: I kept my eyes open so long as I could, and even commenced to count the hairs that were left in the comb from the last time I dressed
20   your hair, in the hope of its entertaining me; but the exertion proved worse than the pleasure, and I fell asleep over it.

Lev. Give me some—some water.

Ida. (*Handing a goblet.*) Here it is, my lady

Lev. (*Takes a mouthful and returns the glass.*) That 25
will do, Ida,—you have been so long with me, that you
have almost learnt to anticipate my wants from the ex‑
pression of my countenance.

Ida. Yes, my lady, and would I had my life over to
serve you, that I might show you how dear you are to me. 30

Enter FRANCIS, R.

Lev. Who is that?
Fran. My voice is my usher.
Lev. (*Raising herself.*) Why, Francis! how glad I am
to see you. (*Extends her hand.*) I have always liked you,
and if I had not, I would now, because you and Alexan‑ 35
der were mutual friends, and whatever he liked is dear
to me. Ida, you may retire. Francis, will you let in a
little of that sun light. (FRANCIS *opens the middle shut‑
ters, and looks out upon the view.*) It must be near sunset?
Fran. Yes, and the moon is already in the heavens. 40
Lev. (*Aside.*) And so it was, when Alexander and my‑
self parted in the garden. (*Aloud.*) What is the hour,
Francis?
Fran. (*Observing his watch.*) It is just half-past six.
Lev. It is the hour, and over, that I should take my 45
powder;—I passed the last fever, and had a tranquil
slumber.
Fran. What sleep have you had, Levangeline?
Lev. I slept from four o'clock till within a few moments
before you entered. 50
Fran. I'll prepare your powders myself, Levangeline:—
you know it would be uncourteous to say the least, if not
unjust, to distrust my ability.
Lev. True, Francis, this is the first time I have seen
you since your promotion to the degree of Doctor of Phi‑ 55
losophy.
Fran. I only returned at three this afternoon.
Lev. How kind and considerate to think of me so
early.
Fran. Don't speak of that now,—if my task, when fully 60
finished, should be proved to have been of value by its
good ends, then I shall find my best reward in the con‑

sciousness of having faithfully served you. (*Mixes the
powders in a glass of water.*)

    Lev. What do you mean by serving me, Francis?

65   *Fran.* Well, to the point, I'm going to take my temporary lodgings at the house whose chimney top is just
peeping on a line with yonder window, and though my
address will be there, my residence is *here* through all
your trials.

70   *Lev.* Oh! Francis, my days will be drawn out in
thanking you;—but I fear my wants will come between
you and your dear ambitious objects too often.

    Fran. This powder is not dissolved sufficiently. (*Shakes
the glass a few times.*)   There,—its last traces have now
75 disappeared. Perhaps I ought to act as the steward
to one of the Roman emperors;—taste the food before
offering it, to prove its quality beyond suspicion.

    Lev. Oh, no; I'm sure it's quite right, if you have
prepared it. (*Drinks the medicine, and returns the glass.*)
80 It's an improvement on the last I took, which could not
have been thoroughly mixed, for it clung to my throat
after I had drank it.—Francis, give me your hand, and
remember my words!—If one day, you should meet a
lonely, handsome, chaste girl that may possess all to
85 make her worthy of yourself, and you should seek her
love, tell her that one who loved you as a brother, would
tell her to take all of you. Now open yonder stand
drawer, and a little to the left, you will find a small key
connected to another by a pink ribbon,—with it open the
90 casket on the bureau top,—and there you will find a like-
ness:—I had it lately taken, and you well know for
whom. If under the patient care, you have so kindly
proffered, I should not linger long, hang it in a treasured
spot within your own apartments, and as often as you
95 look upon it, think of one that regarded you as *I* do!

    Fran. I'll keep it amongst my choicest jewels of the
kind.

    Lev. And more,—the day that Alexander and myself
were strolling in the garden, just the same hour, and
100 much the same weather too as this, I wore upon my left
breast a delicate mimosa, a piece of which I gave to him
on parting, the rest I have ever since preserved, still fresh

and blooming in yonder little vase. If, as I said before, I should not linger long under your faithful service, bury them with me, and strew my grave with leaves of others 105 like those my mother planted on my father's grave; and perhaps chance or the wind will cast a few of the seeds of some of them amidst the grass which shall cover *his own!*

Fran. Levangeline! you must not broach such thoughts. I am a sensitive disposition, and you would be the means 110 of my losing faith in my own services. I did not enter life by dealing in improbabilities, much less impossibilities. Mark me,—you are yet to be happy, but I know as little of the means, as the little that your faith depends on. 115

Lev. Will you draw to the left shutter, the light strikes my eyes?

Fran. (*Goes to the window, and closes the left inside shutter, at the same time looking out upon the road.*) I descry a cloud of dust, from which I observe Frederick to prick forth on horseback, as it rolls on towards the 120 house. I suppose he is on some errand of compassion, you know he has relinquished the world, and has offered himself to it as a friend to misery. He has not turned the corner—forsooth he is nearing here. I'll leave you for a moment, and will place the alarum within your 125 grasp, in case you should be suddenly in want of any thing. [*Places a hand bell on the couch. Exit, R.*

Lev. He is not designed for this world:—I'm sure such a devoted, disinterested heart, aspiring soul, will be abused on this cold earth. Now that letter, whose seal I 130 never yet have had the courage to break.

[*She rises on the couch, makes a few steps, and is obliged to pause; then resumes her steps, and reaches the window, R., after some exertion, which she opens; seats herself, and looks out into the street. A peal is heard from the chimes of the Cathedral, which is supposed to be directly opposite, intermingled with the tones of the organ.*

It is a holyday in the Church, Good-Friday, and there are the pious souls wending their way to Vespers. It is

Good-Friday ! and distant only two days from Easter,
135 the day on which three years ago, I left the Convent.
'Twere better I *never* had.—Oh ! that was a cruel thought,
for how well purchased were those few days of bliss,
though at the price of the life of misery I now lead.
(*Goes to the stand, opens the drawer, takes out a letter,
drops it, picks it up, breaks it open, and reads.*) "It is
140 midnight now. All the world is hushed around me, and
I am possessed of calmness I know not how ! Levangeline, I have just opened my eyes on the heavens, and
through a faint breach in a dense cloud that was just
passing over my window, I saw some stars, and amongst
145 the others Vesper, the Evening Star, it is a beautiful
name, and one of the favorites too with the astronomer,—
it was this that shone upon us at our last parting in the
garden, and on which I have often since looked with rap-
ture, and made it a witness of our past felicity ! I see
150 you in it as I do in all things that make life dear to me.
You are, therefore, even with me now. Levangeline ! I am
obliged to a friend for noting these my freshest thoughts."

[*She drops the letter, and remains for some moments in a
state of mental stupefaction, then starts up with a shriek.*

Re-enter FRANCIS, R.

Fran. Levangeline ! how came you there?
Lev. By my resolution.
155 *Fran.* There's strange news abroad !
Lev. Strange news !
Fran. Yes, what you would least believe, but would
most wish true for your own happiness.
Lev. (*Raising herself.*) Do not taunt me thus with
160 base deception;—
Thy eye something foretells ;—thy tongue says nothing.
Fran. Alexander lives !
Lev.   He lives ! [*Falling on him.*
Fran.   Ay, truly.
165 *Lev.* If he still lives, wherefore said'st thou he died ?
Fran. Levangeline ! you soon shall learn the whole ;
For Frederick's come, full of haste and joy.

Enter FREDERICK, R.

Lev. He lives! speak it again! Speak it again!
It comes to me each time with new born freshness,
As an untold tale! Speak it again!   170
Let me be sure of it,—for I'm carried
In exstacy beyond my senses!
If it be true, I'll fall and worship thee;
'Tis the pride of thy dear philosophy
To speak consolation to distracted spirits,   175
And mine is one of them.
Speak it again! does Alexander live?
  Fred. Keep in calmness while I speak.
  Lev.   Speak at once,—
I hang upon the utterance of thy lips,   180
Drinking their accents, though they should prove vain.
  Fred. As I was about leaving the body of our friend
for a short absence, I thought I observed something
seeming much like a muscular contraction,—when, aided
by this little glass which I hold in my hand, (*Exhibiting* 185
a watch glass,) by placing it quite over his lips, and keeping it thus arranged for a few seconds, I removed it to
where the light shone bright upon it, when I witnessed
that the glass was become slightly clouded by a dense
moisture,—which was in truth his own condensed breath. 190
I lost no moments in questioning the rightful authority,
his own physician, when, on my return, I found that he
had even provided for his doom,—for according to his
sealed instructions, directed to me, his body was to be
buried by four household menials, accompanied by a sole 195
priest, and his own faithful valet,—and after the first day
to be reduced to ashes, enclosed in a silver urn, fashioned
as a broken anchor, and thus finally interred in the manner that his friends should agree on.
  Lev. Oh! let me thank thee, who hast thus saved him, 200
Whose life was part of mine; and though languishing
Faintness forbids me more to express,
My heart would tell thee, I'm grateful to thee!
I ever thought thee to be more than friendly,
And if thou art thus empowered, grant me this!—   205
Bring him I love, one moment, lest I die.

[FREDERICK *nods assent, and exits,* R., FRANCIS *helps her to a seat, then exits,* R.

Ay, I will, must see him while I may live.
My love! haste, a word might kill me outright.—
Those hollow footsteps on the outer hall!
210 I hear him;—he is come;—it is he! it is he!

ALEXANDER *enters unobserved by* LEVANGELINE.

Alex. Levangeline!
Lev.   That voice! it is still his own!
                    [*They rush into an embrace.*
Alex. Levangeline! thou art mine!
My love! my joy! my world! sum of my life,
215 Thought of my thoughts,—thy smiles my blessings!
In a sad hour I dreamt of a future
That did not wear thy love,—Thou'st still been faithful:
Henceforth, our lives are one for evermore!
Lev. Which, say but which of you shall I kneel to,—
220 Thou, who art spared to me, or he who by
Thus saving thy life, in that has saved mine!
Alex. Let us talk of joy,—joy, Levangeline.
Let us banish the past whose grim visage
Falls on us with such deep and hideous blackness.
225 We'll fly to the future,—to the morrow.
By to-morrow morn's dawn, if thou shouldst chose,
Our clasping hands shall meet by the altar,
As waves upon the shore, that part no more.
Lev. Ah, yes; but there will be an eternity
230 Before the morrow.
Alex.   But think not on it,
Levangeline! and 'twill steal upon us,
As the midnight hymn, on that beauteous night,
When we were seated beneath thy lattice,
235 In speechless intercourse, listening to all
Creation syllabing our tales of love.
Lev. It is but evening yet—the sun hath
Just fell golden on his pavilioned arch—
The moon sits like a white beacon of light
240 In the darkening silence of twilight—

The restless breeze doth gently sway the trees,
Rocking to rest the birds that build upon them.
Do not thus come to speak of the morrow
With power in thyself to scare off Time's hand.
    Alex. The sun no more shall look on us in sorrow ;—   245
The night is nigh. Would we might be empowered,
To move the dial without waiting its return.
    Lev. Yet I do weep to see the day die out ;
The death-knell of a day, how beautiful !—
A short time since, I woke as from a dream,   250
And fancied that thou hadst come to see me.
Thou saw'st me—flew to me—half out of breath ;
Thy hand was on my arm—thou kissed me oft,
And put my long black locks backwards.
I dreamt—and woke—and then methought,—alas !   255
'Tis but a dream—those arms will never fold me.
    Alex. Without, without, I'll tell thee much without.
             [ALEXANDER *leads her off,* R.

         Enter IDA, L.

    Ida. (C.) The bed chamber is empty ; my lady
Is not here to be found ! The Count Francis too,
Who watched near her, is gone too. If she should   260
Have fled—but wherefore fled ? I must call up
The menials of the house. I think I hear
Voices and footsteps below ! I will go,
And listen without the door. Hark, who is that ?
I hear the pacing of steps through the hall.   [*Exit,* R.   **265**

SCENE II.—*The liquor vaults in the mansion of* COUNT
    MANDERSTEM ; *barrels, baskets, and flasks strewed
    throughout the apartment.*

Enter FRANCIS, FREDERICK, *and the* BUTLER, *followed by*
    MICHAEL, ALFRED, *and Servants.* FRANCIS *and* FREDE-
    RICK *come forward,* R. C. BUTLER, MICHAEL, *and* AL-
    FRED, C. *as in conversation. Servants pass to and fro in
    the rear.*

    Fran. If the old Count and his lady could but see these

strange issues to their preconceived plans, their very vaults would echo with their bodies turning over on their couches.

270 *Fred.* Yes, yes, my lord. It is but true there never was a story of more mysterious turns, and such an unexpected end, than this we have each witnessed. But I fear this connection however agreeable to themselves, and pleasing to us, looks forward to no good.

275 *Fran.* That is ——

Fred. It is attained under the most unpropitious circumstances.

Fran. Heaven forbid. Never did a marriage, under such peculiar conditions too, seem to offer a brighter pros-
280 pect.

Fred. Well, well,—if those are your thoughts, be contented to remain by them.

Fran. Yes, for I am the better persuaded of it on this head,—had I not ventured, even against my own convic-
285 tions, the kind deception allowed to all physicians, and giving her the appeasing assurance that convalescence was not far distant, and with it speedy recovery to hopes unknown,—she would never have been braced in spirit against her bodily weakness to leave this mansion for the
290 altar before the hour of the morning mass.

Fred. Though the Church would tell you, there's nothing like religion for a wounded spirit.

Fran. I well knew *that*, and lost no time to prepare myself against the dogmas of those scalp-headed Carmelites,
295 that would have taught her, shut in a cloister, to treasure every moment of her life,—to pray for the lengthening of her days, that by fasting, tears, and midnight chilling prayers, she could draw out her days, till every ray of hope was spent,—then at the end to say, you may now
300 die, for you have well grieved enough.

Enter MICHAEL, L.

Mich. Friar William awaits, and would have a word with your lordship.

Fred. Ask his reverence to come *below.*

[*Exit* MICHAEL, L.

Fran. Yes, ask him to see us *here,*—for if the apartment is fitted for a Baron and a Doctor of Philosophy, it   305
is enough so for his reverence.

Fred. (*To the* BUTLER.) Have a flowing bowl in readiness, and I'll warrant that you'll receive plenty of abso-
lution in return.

[FREDERICK *and* FRANCIS *walk aside as in conversation.*

Butler. The best of wine the vaults can afford—a bottle   310
of the last fifty years vintage of Madeira or Port,—and
add one of Rhenish from the Count's own possessions.—
Let's try that cask of Cognac to the left.   (*Servants roll
a cask down,* C.)   Now, the further one to the right. Why
do you stand loitering there?—I'll find if you have any   315
hearing presently—that cask that stands furthest to the
right.   Look you to the Champagne cases, and examine
if none of the flasks be broken; (*the Servants bring forward a case of Champagne wine* ;) see, there's one broken
before your eyes.   320

Re-enter MICHAEL, L.

Mich. His reverence, Friar William approaches.

Enter FRIAR WILLIAM, L.

Friar. Benedicite vos.

Fred. Good evening to your reverence.

Friar. Have your lordships nigh prepared for the morrow's nuptial ceremonies?   325

Fred. They are well nigh prepared, your reverence,—
all to the decking of the festal halls.

Friar. I have come at this late hour of the day, to see
that we have brought into use on the morrow, the bowl
with which the punch was served at our Lady's christen-   330
ing ceremony.

Fred. (*To the* BUTLER.) Do you know the vessel?

Butler. Ay, well, my lord. (*Aside to Servant.* Bring me
the bowl that lies in the case on the upper shelf of the
plate room.   335

Fran. (*To the* FRIAR.) The Butler has ordered the
vessel to be brought hither.   He says it is well known to
him.

Butler. Ay, it was first used on the occasion of the
340 marriage of her ladyship's father,—and there's not another
piece more precious in the whole contents of the closets.

Re-enter SERVANT, L., *with the bowl.*

Fran. Is that the one your reverence used at the
christening of her ladyship, eighteen years ago?
Friar. (*Examining the bowl.*) Ay, the same.
345 *Mich.* (*Aside to* ALFRED.) This will be something to
figure in the Vienna Zeitung.
Fred. Allow me to have a look at it. (*Handles it.*) It
is a rare gem, indeed, and how heavy too.
Fran. As well it may be, for it is solid gold,—judging
350 by its weight, as compared with its size.
Fred. And what neat chasing is embossed upon its
outside. How natural and elegant is this figure; yet one
cannot divest himself of the thought, that it bears a like-
ness to the panel paintings executed on the chancel doors
355 by the friars of old; while the paintings outside the door
represented the passion of our Lord, the inside pictured
wantonness by representing the loves of Cupid and Venus.
So in this vessel, while the chasing illustrates the Passion
of our Lord, its contents, or the punch, would denote a
360 source of revelry.
Fran. Let's have a toast.
Fred. To beauty's fairest flowers,—Alexander and
Levangeline, the offspring of our birthland.
Fran. Be it so! a glorious toast.
365 *Fred.* I cannot drink the toast, that I have given, for
fear of drinking to the dead.
Fran. Then have out upon your conscience; and drink
though it be but to drown its officious preachings within.
Friar Will. Life's pleasures are a battle of long date,
370 and when they're won, we grasp for the bright bubble,
which breaks in its rise. [*They drink the toast. Exeunt*
FRIAR WILLIAM, FREDERICK, *and* FRANCIS, R.
Butler. (*As he is going off.*) Of what shall I sing?
Mich. Of any thing merry,—of wine.
Butler. (*Sings.*)

While the wine's flowing,
The senses are glowing,
As lightly as the cork floating,
On the beer froth o'erflowing.

[*Exeunt* MICHAEL *and* ALFRED, L.: BUTLER *and* SER-
  VANTS, R.

SCENE III.—*The interior of the Cathedral; banners
bearing the coat armor of families on either side; a
monument to the memory of the* MANDERSTEM *family,* R.
C.; *another bearing the name of* WIED *further back.*

LEVANGELINE *and* ALEXANDER *discovered kneeling before
the altar,* C., *as at the close of the marriage service, before
whom stands* FRIAR WILLIAM; *after which they approach
near front of stage,* C. *preceded by* FRIAR WILLIAM
LEVANGELINE *faulters and falls into* ALEXANDER'S *arms,
where she remains for some moments in speechless
embrace.*

Lev. Oh!
Alex.   Levangeline!   375
Lev. (*With an effort.*)   Alexander!
Do not be unwilling to hear me!
Alex. Wherefore should I?
Lev.   Thou wilt surely be!
Alex. Thy silent look has killing sounds foretold.   380
But speak,—speak the mournful'st thought thou hast,
While I gaze on thine eyes, thou seem'st to me
As the stars in the prisoner's dark'ned cell:
Thus would I drink the music of thy voice,
And if its words should prove poison's own draught,   385
There may be richest pleasure in its dregs.
  Lev. Hither we're come to take our last farewell;—
For life's billows are fast breaking o'er me,
Steeped in the sunlight of eternity!
I feel that I am going!   390
  Alex.   Not dying!
  Lev. Ah, yes,—nearer,—there's something I would tell,
Ere we part for evermore, but not forever.

For we shall yet meet in spite of sorrows,
395 At last in heaven,—thus forget the past:
And if the fate of her by thee beloved
Doth cause one grief, then think she suffers nought :—
But if, perchance, thou wilt weep still, then think
That love's thy fancied sorrow, and live to
400 Love the dead, and me whose spirit shall live
In peace, and saint-like purity, and prayer;
And then, when, thine shall fly afar from earth, ·
I'll pray to heaven, that it may join mine there.
    Alex. I cannot—dare not, look upon thee, love !
405 For fear of looking on the dying.
    Lev. Speak to me as to the dying, my best loved !
The dead are never faithless—dost hear me ?
    Alex. Thus,—thus, art thou punished for others' wrongs.
    Lev. You were my life, but death triumphs o'er it.
410   *Alex* Forbear,—forbear, to further pierce this stricken
    breast.
Oh heav'n and earth ! should'st thou resolve to die,
And tear all beauty from this widowed earth,
Then let a couch of lead, let death's cold mantle,
415 And the earth's tall grass together hold us ;
Ere such a fate shall on my life be come,
For in death alone I should find peace.
    Lev. (*In broken accents*) Alexander ! still here ! Oh,
    killing joy !
420 · Am I alive ! is this delirium !
'Tis he, 'tis my best loved lover,—husband !
(*Sinking.*) Thou art fast,—fast vanishing from my sight,
Let me feel thee still,—my heart would tell thee more,—
It breaks, it melts,—it is not adamant !
    Alex. (*With his whole form expressive of a sudden out-*
    burst of anguish, raises his eyes, and falls by the
425   *side of* LEVANGELINE.) Levangeline ! Levangeline !
Still deeper be my life atoned for thine !
    Lev. I am passing away—changing scenes—
Is this death—then life's a dream—I see birds
Of ever varying plumes, yonder—I hear
430 The rustling of breezes fanned by angel wings—
'Tis spring time—leaves have no time of falling there—
They're talking of things past, present, and to come—

I am so cold—strew leaves over me.
(*Looks into the face of* ALEXANDER *for a moment, and*
        holds out her hand to him.) Come !   [*Dies.*
  Friar. Help ! help ! support him !   435
  Alex.   Nay, nay, 'tis too late !
In a few moments has my fate been sealed,
And with it thus soon my life's accomplished.
This much in death be granted us—one sepulchre.
Hard by the sepulchres of our forefathers.   440
  Friar. I will, and more, a tablet to thee raise,
Of deeds as noble as thou hast early achieved ;
There peaceful be the sleep of this fair pair,
Than whom none brighter ere on earth have shone.
Pure fame, true beauty, with transcendant worth,   445
Rude stone ! beneath thy lettered breast be laid—
Go hence, to others speak of these sad things.
O house of death and sorrows !—it seems to me
A very charnel hall, with rooms dressed up,
With the lean gloom that melancholy wears.   450
                        [*Exit Friar.*

THE CURTAIN FALLS.

Philadelphia :—Printed by King & Baird.

www.ingramcontent.com/pod-product-compliance
Lightning Source LLC
Chambersburg PA
CBHW030007030726
47499CB00008B/2935